MISSING IN

MUMBAI

A RUDHRANI SEN MYSTERY

KIRKI AKRIVOU

LINGUIST MAGAZINE PRESS

For all those who struggle to balance expectations with personal purpose.

REAL QUICK

Before you get started, get a free mystery story, raffles, and discounts on upcoming titles at www.kirkiakrivou.com/newsletter

Contents

THE MISSING

RUDHRANI

WHEN RUDHRANI SEN AGREED to return to India in the throes of the monsoon season for a hastily planned wedding, she did not expect to be hired to solve a missing persons case and probable murder.

But as it happened, her cousin's best friend's sister's roommate from Mumbai found herself in a bizarre situation. A friend from a neighboring housing society now living in London, Asha Khan, had asked the young woman to check on her mother, whom she hadn't been able to reach for days. Asha would come herself, but she had been injured in a traffic accident and could barely walk.

Given that it was just down the street, the dutiful friend had agreed. After haranguing the watchman and the building's manager, she was finally able to enter the flat, which was entirely empty.

Her cousin Amrita described the situation while sampling the wedding caterer's appetizers. In fact, she said dramatically, the roommate had noted that it hadn't looked like anyone had been inside for a few days. Food was left out, the bananas were rotten, and laundry remained damp at the bottom of a 20-year-old Whirlpool washer.

"Baba always says you're good at solving things," the round-faced girl said, leaning her chin on her henna-adorned hand. "What do you think of this?"

While her uncle was a great detective, his daughter failed to take an interest in sleuthing herself. Rudhrani, however, savored every mystery—from strange noises outside her window to abnormal ultrasounds and MRIs as a radiologist to her part-time private investigation hustle.

"I think I'd have to know more. It could be Mrs. Khan realized her groceries were going bad and left to get some more."

Her cousin frowned, dissatisfied. "Well, I think it sounds odd. I mean, if your daughter was in London, wouldn't you at least call them back when you returned home? And she said that her mother didn't call her for days. How often do you speak to your parents from America?"

Fair point. Of course, the two could have gotten into a fight. Perhaps, in reality, they had a poor relationship. Really, the entire 'case' could just be an extended game of telephone.

But still, when she should have been recovering from her thirty-hour trip to Kolkata, Rudhrani couldn't help herself. She wanted, like her cousin, to know more. At the very least, she could validate her ideas with a few questions.

"You wouldn't happen to have the roommate's number, by any chance?"

"Oh, I can get it," Amrita smiled widely. "But only if you promise to work on it *after* the wedding."

The part-time sleuth promised, although that didn't stop her from contacting the roommate. Or getting Asha Khan's number. Or agreeing to investigate after hearing that not only was Asha's mother in good mental and physical health but that she had complained of being followed. The festivities didn't even stop her from conducting cursory research as she gobbled down as many delicacies as possible at the reception.

And, leaving her brother to care for her parents, Rudhrani boarded a plane a week early to fly west across the country to the sprawling metropolis of Mumbai.

The Untenable Inheritance

Shonali

ALL SHONALI CHATTERJEE SAW for kilometers was a thick cloak of fog and vague wisps of hillside silhouettes. Their gargantuan shadows towered over the twisted road, like stone walls over a prisoner. The vast and curvaceous valley sighed in the absence of clear blue summer skies, sputtering a somber monsoon drizzle. It was, theoretically, the best time to visit the hill stations of Maharashtra—but the worst time to visit its capital, Mumbai.

Unfortunately, Shonali's destination was the latter. There would be no quiet retreats to Lonavala, no rest in hilltop spas, or lounging in a hotel room suite with strong cardamom chai. Instead, the young woman found herself saddled at a way station, rehearsing her upcoming itinerary for her time in the sprawling city.

The last time Shonali traversed the Mumbai-Pune expressway was well over a decade ago, near the end of her childhood, her large eyes captivated by the Ghats, the grassy giants cloaked in a veil of awe. But now at twenty-five years old and amid the early-morning monsoon fog, that long-held nostalgia held within it a rooted unease. This was a trip she never wanted to make and a situation she never wanted to be in.

Nevertheless, here she was.

While her father rested, immobile and mute after his stroke, and her brother toiled in sunny California, Shonali held the responsibility of managing an inherited rental flat in one of the most luxurious districts of Mumbai. And she was failing at it. Miserably.

Shonali shivered at the faint trill of the macaques and the crows shrieking back at them. From her past travels, she remembered those small monkeys on the roadside, pillaging through a shredded bag of oranges, looking sweet, if a bit mischievous, as they watched the cars speed past with their round eyes.

But while she heard their irate cries, the barely visible road and parking lot outside of Woodstock Food Mall remained empty of life, animal or otherwise.

The desolate roads were for the better. Just an hour outside of Pune, Shonali was making good time. That was largely due to the subpar weather conditions, keeping potential tourists off the roads, and the regular heavy downpours flooding the western coast. On account of her driver not having eaten, Shonali decided to stop at the way station.

How she had let her brother convince her to splurge on a private driver to Mumbai, she wasn't sure. *"It'll be safer, faster,"* he had pleaded when she mentioned booking the train. He wasn't wrong. And even though her bank account was close to collapsing and her credit essentially overextended, Shonali was grateful for the comfort and flexibility of her car ride and for being able to get out and stretch her legs.

She ordered a thumb-sized paper cup of chai from a small stall in the back of the food court and paced around the back of the building. It was too early to call the tenants. Shonali wasn't even sure if they knew she was coming.

She wished that they'd responded to her text message the week before. Then, perhaps, she could have saved money and time and returned home for work. Instead, she had to squint at her mobile screen and make grammar corrections to articles during the car ride—articles from which she wouldn't see a rupee for at least another 90 days. But it would arrive, eventually.

Yet even now, Shonali could barely focus on the words, already exhausted from all the late nights, the early mornings, and the cold grasp of anxiety on her heart. The gradually diminishing funds in her bank account kept her up at night. Her new boss didn't help.

Ever since Shonali's last editor left her position at the small, local rag she worked at, and the paper had been subsequently bought, her life had been hell. While she had been only an entry-level proofreader, her last boss often indulged Shonali's journalistic endeavors. Now, every proofreading recommendation was scrutinized, every stylistic comment opened to harsh criticism, and she was strictly barred from venturing outside her responsibilities on her own.

But after two years of chronic unemployment and the staggering amount of effort it took to land her current job, she had little interest in leaving it. There was no guarantee of "something better." As her brother's remittances grew smaller and smaller each month, it was clear that Shonali would need to continue working to support their father.

Her eyes focused on the fog, a gossamer morning mist that cloaked the green curves of the Ghats. At least it wasn't a complete downpour, although it had already rained much in the area, softening the earth and increasing the likelihood of mudslides.

Throwing her teacup in a dustbin, she decided to try the restroom before heading back to the car.

The travelers were few and far between, meaning there wasn't even a queue. She peeked behind the stalls—one western toilet and two traditional ones, only one door locked, and every stall coated with thick, black mold.

Unsurprised yet still unsettled, Shonali finished her business quickly and washed her hands. Without a paper towel, she patted her pink cotton dupatta and headed for the car.

It was then that her phone vibrated. Her brother. Glancing at the time, she decided she could spare a few minutes.

"Ajit, isn't it late there?" She tried to sound caring but stern. Anything but exhausted.

"Not at all," her brother said, his jovial voice ringing with static. "Only six thirty in the evening. Where are you?"

"We stopped at the hill station. The driver hadn't eaten at all."

"You're too soft with people," her brother muttered quietly. "You did book it through a proper agency, didn't you? I sent enough. Did the tenants get in touch with you?"

Despite being a software engineer, the concept of inflation and the cost of her father's care seemed to bypass her brother entirely, so he had sent a meager amount that barely covered half of the driver's fee. Shonali had footed the rest. She bit her tongue. Aggression would only drive him away, as any criticism did.

So, she focused on the problem at hand.

"No, but I left another WhatsApp message for the Bharadwajs." Shonali sighed. "I told you we shouldn't have taken them."

"Relax, relax. They'll pay the rent. They're good people, after all. The broker vetted them. I vetted them. I'm sure it's just a misunderstanding."

Shonali wanted to probe him further. She knew what he meant by good people, but she hardly agreed with his increasingly narrow definition of what constituted an upstanding citizen. When he had deviated into moralistic judgments, she wasn't sure. Perhaps all those extra tuition hours, the hard slap of humiliation after every failed exam, now incited him to cleave the world into two halves: the successful and the mistakes.

When Ajit had returned in a rush from Mumbai a year ago, she had considered he was just eager to finish the laborious work of finding a suitable tenant for their uncompromising flat. His agreement to rent to the Bharadwajs was almost instant. But Shonali had reasoned that Ajit had been entirely absorbed by his work in California, just as she was focused on finding work and supporting their father. Rather than account for every single possibility, isn't it better to latch onto an opportunity?

To her thirty-five-year-old brother, their broker landed a "dream" renter situation, a family of good means. Educated, wealthy, and polite, they simply wanted a small apartment to live in when conducting business in the area. Ajit appeared to be successful at property management and boasted about it often. But besides signing the papers, he had little to do with the actual process. And since, according to Ajit, their broker left Mumbai shortly afterward, the responsibility for the flat fell on Shonali's bony shoulders.

Massaging her temples, Shonali couldn't help but wonder *why* her parents had never sold the flat when capital gains taxes were easier to avoid and the list of required documentation more flexible. She wanted to ask her brother now, while he was on the line, why he didn't just sell it before he left.

Their paltry one-bedroom flat was hardly fit for bachelors and students—their normal average renters—who often left it trashed and unpainted. But this was a family, and a family of a certain pedigree, although that was true of all of their tenants. The complex in Worli was hardly affordable for most families, and the size of each flat hardly allowed for sub-leasing. And despite its age, their property, as unappealing and prone to leaks as it was, demanded higher rent from its ideal location. Its quaint charm attracted the wealthy, who were often looking for a short-term residence for business or studies.

"Are you there, Shonali? You're not losing it, are you?"

"Losing it, what do you mean?"

"You know what I mean," she heard her brother grumble. "You got all worked up during 10th standard exams and nearly gave Baba a heart attack with your antics. Same thing when Ma died."

"I'm *fine,*" Shonali stressed, even though she wasn't. And why should she be?

They were barely breaking even with the rental income. After Ajit left for his new, but not exactly lucrative, job abroad, Shonali had sat down, rummaged through the finances, and added estate management to her never-ending list of duties.

Higher rent, Shonali had soon discovered, did not translate into profits or savings. The cost of maintenance, utilities, and regular repairs devoured the majority of the cost. And the flat, as small and aged as it was, was already priced at its acceptable limit. Even raising rent by a thousand rupees would likely drive away any and all tenants—unless black money was involved.

The rental documentation, clumsily signed and tucked away, still lay in disorganized heaps and manila folders in a teak cabinet. But she had gleaned enough from past bills to construct a spreadsheet and realized how untenable the inheritance had become. Renting the flat provided a measly 2,000 rupees[1] to the household per month, but it could cover most of the Pune bills if they defaulted on its maintenance payments.

Despite the small influx of cash, Shonali couldn't help but wonder if the paltry remainder was worth the effort. But defaulting wasn't an option. Not if she ever wanted to sell the Mumbai flat.

---

1. 2,000 rupees – About 24 USD as of 2023.

"I'm sure you're right," she agreed hesitantly.

From the way her brother had recounted the meeting, he had merely spoken with Raj Bharadwaj—the husband and head of the household—over the phone and was already quite set about offering them the tenancy.

At the time, overloaded with work and taking care of their father, Shonali had consented, attributing her inhibitions to irrationality. Now, the Bharadwajs hadn't paid for over three months and refused to answer her calls. Combined with her erratic payment schedule at the paper, her account was almost always close to empty.

"How is Baba? The same?"

"Fine, fine. I've hired Toral Mausi[2] to stay with him. But Ajit, I may need more money to make it work in case I can't get the payment on this trip."

"I'm sure it'll be fine, Shonali," her brother said flatly. "I'll see what I can do tomorrow. Just see what the situation is first. I've got to go. Message me later!"

The line beeped, and suddenly, she was alone again.

Twisting her braid around her finger, Shonali started back toward the car. The food mall was barren, and travelers were sparse. Shonali noticed the driver, Siddharth Thetwar, was by the car, leaning against it leisurely, spooning channa masala[3] into his mouth slowly,

---

2. Mausi - The term for maternal aunt, often used in Hindi and Marathi when addressing both your actual aunt or women who are domestic workers.

3. Channa Masala - It's a chickpea dish. Highly recommend.

savoring each bite. But as he noticed her walking toward the car, he hurriedly finished his meal, tossed it into a plastic bag, and started the Maruti hatchback.

The radio squeaked on, and Jagjit Singh's voice wafted through the speakers as Shonali approached, a drizzle of rain coating her hair and ears. A crow cawed incessantly, closer than it had been before as if its beak might clip her ear. She glanced over her shoulder, but there was only gravel—and a few cars with muddied bumpers.

Sliding into the hatchback's backseat, Shonali checked her phone again. Another missed call from an unknown number. A few promotional text messages. But nothing from her tenants.

The Bharadwaj family maintained their silence.

THE GOLDEN DEER

SHONALI

N EARLY TWO HOURS CRAWLED by as Shonali suffered through bumper-to-bumper traffic, traveling from Navi Mumbai to what her parents and brother considered "a marvelous status of hard-earned wealth"—a dilapidated, single-bedroom flat on the top floor of a five-story building in Worli.

Unlike the luxurious high-rises dominating this side of the city, the Golden Deer Housing Society[1] comprised two crumbling, lift-less buildings. In its heyday, it had been a sound, cozy middle-class complex with a thin golden coat of paint that almost reflected the sun. The paint had faded, peeled, and cracked into a dull brownish beige.

From her family's photographs, the surrounding, similarly aged flats had been bought out shortly after their family moved to

---

1. Co-op Housing Society - This is exactly what it sounds like. A cooperative housing society is essentially a residential complex (although the ground floor may have shops) that is run by the residents. There is no single "owner" so to speak.

Pune. The developers had demolished the sixties-era residences and replaced them with towering modern complexes hosting every potential amenity the mind could imagine.

Now, in an isolated plot surrounded by twenty-story high-rises, the Golden Deer complex stood the two lonely buildings, each crudely repainted creature cracked and cobbled together with superficial facelifts. Its proximity to the beach and the Bandra-Worli Sea Link elevated the small, decrepit flat to prime real estate, driving rent, tax, and maintenance costs up.

But Shonali knew, without a doubt, that if those same developers took hold of the land, they would only turn it into a garden or a waste pit. The land was too old, too small to do anything worthwhile. In short, it was almost worthless.

As they approached the aging society, the sprawling peepal tree[2] that shaded the front gate offered Shonali a brief glimpse of her childhood: Neighbors visiting during Diwali, purpled faces of other children colored with Holi powder, a stray cat licking its paws beneath her father's new Maruti Alto. And, of course, heated arguments between her mother and father, her father and his brother, their voices rising like the whistle of a pressure cooker.

Shonali assumed that the neighbors had not changed since her family had moved. Before his stroke, her father had taken the time to meet with them every time there was a new tenant—if only to remain in the committee's good graces and increase his leverage whenever he eventually sold the flat.

---

2. Peepal tree - A type of fig tree

The co-op was a retirement village at this point, a monument to the diversity and style of twentieth-century Mumbai. The names and flat numbers rested on her tongue: Deshpande, Yadav, Khan, Kabraji, Singh, Rao, Desai... The aunties and uncles of her youth, in her eyes, served almost as supplemental family members, replacing the estranged relatives she rarely met except in moments of anger.

And so, when she entered the society, Shonali was comforted to see Pooja Desai, the committee chairwoman, where she had always been—out on the grounds, the watchman lounging in a plastic chair behind her.

Pooja was a woman of considerable age, but rather than littered with wrinkles, her face smiled with a graceful roundness. She had full cheeks, henna-colored, shoulder-length thick hair, and simple, golden earrings. Shonali had no doubt they were real gold, the metal shimmering in the noon light.

Today, Pooja stood at the foot of her building, petting a stray dog, the edge of her muted orange dupatta barely skimming the pavement. The dog thrust its head against the woman's plump fingers eagerly, tongue lolling out between crusted lips. Her kajal-rimmed eyes shot to Shonali's car as soon as it entered the gate.

Shaking off the stiffness from the car ride, Shonali climbed out of the hatchback and stretched, smiling at Pooja. Now that the woman had seen her, it was better to make a good impression. Besides, Shonali knew that she might be able to glean some information about her unresponsive tenants.

"Ah, Shonali beta[3]. I didn't expect to see you here. Where is your brother?" Pooja looked over Shonali's shoulder as if she expected Ajit to pop out of the car. If she was disappointed at his absence, Shonali couldn't be sure. Ajit had been childhood friends with her son—it was only natural that the woman preferred his presence to Shonali's.

"He's abroad only, Auntie. It is so good to see you. I am here to check up on my tenants."

"And your father? Leaving him alone?" Pooja asked as she stood at full height, leaving the dog. The wet stray whined and rubbed his head against the woman's casual salwar. Clicking her tongue, Pooja tried to shoo him away.

"Oh, he isn't alone," Shonali said slowly, watching the woman shower the stray with affection once again. "I hope we can meet later. I've brought some cakes from the Kayani Bakery." Shonali dug out a plastic-wrapped walnut cake from her purse and offered it to Pooja with both hands.

"Oh, I would love that! It's been so long since I've visited Pune," Pooja said. Her smile had waned, and her voice wavered. "I do love these cakes. My brother used to bring them during Diwali...You've picked quite good tenants this time, you know. They've followed every rule. Families are so much better than a bachelor or a university

---

3. Beta - This is often used informally to denote someone younger in age. It technically means "son" but is often applied to young women and girls as well.

girl. So much more responsible," Pooja rattled, her fleshy fingers petting the dog roughly behind the ears.

"I'm glad. The Bharadwajs have been no issue at all?"

"No. Quite the opposite," Pooja commented stiffly, glancing up at Shonali. "Quite helpful, in fact. Why do you ask?"

"Oh, no reason. I just haven't been able to get a hold of them."

"Well, you know, the husband, Raj, he's busy so often. In and out all day. And Gita spends all her time cooking and volunteering."

"Is that so?"

"Yes," Pooja said quietly. Standing up again and leaving the dog to whine, she studied Shonali. "They are both quite busy. And their son stays with them often. He's working, I believe, in the family business. I'm sure everything just got lost in the shuffle. Especially now."

Shonali blinked, surprised to hear that all three shared a minuscule, one-bedroom flat, especially since they were wealthy and had a permanent home elsewhere.

"What's happening now?"

"Nothing, really," Pooja said quickly. "Just that Gita told me that she likes to start Diwali cleaning early. She's probably been preoccupied."

"Ah, I see. I'll stop by later, then, Pooja Auntie." Shonali excused herself and ascended the tight, cream-colored staircase.

Diwali cleaning her ass.

If Shonali could answer text messages while working full-time, caring for her father, and maintaining the household, Gita

Bharadwaj could leave a quick update or even an excuse about their unpaid rent.

The more she thought about it, the angrier she became, and she had plenty of time to fume while climbing the stairway to the fifth floor.

The Golden Deer lacked a lift. Residents relied solely upon a narrow series of stairs, with a Mughal-styled mesh wall filtering the light in the shape of flowers. Or at least that is what it had been. What was in its place now only added to her dismay.

The ornamental siding had vanished, crudely replaced with cement for a gray wall and a generic white fluorescent lightbulb. Only a tiny sliver—the topmost portion of the wall, where a long slit was made as a window and decorative border—remained. Shonali's lips pursed at the sight, remembering lazy afternoons spent in the shade of these stairs, sprawled on the floor with a book, underlining every word touched by the light.

But now, at high noon, darkness drenched every step.

Clicking her tongue, Shonali held the cool metal railing and, step by step, began to recite the prepared, assertive speech she had rehearsed the night before. Every turn made her stomach curl, her mouth dry, and her hands clammy and cold.

You can do this, Shonali. She crossed the first floor. *Everything will be okay.*

— ◆ —

The Flat

Shonali

WHEN SHONALI REACHED THE fifth floor, she paused in front of her flat, Number 501. She found the entire entrance unfamiliar. The simple lattice iron exterior door had been replaced with a thick sheet of steel sprayed with a gray liquid metal. It looked like a vault.

The wooden plaque with her father's name had been removed. To the right of the door was now a steel sign with the names of her tenants engraved beside an orange swastik: Mr. and Mrs. Raj Bharadwaj.

An immense feeling of encroachment swelled in her chest. They should have at least called about the changes to the flat. She wouldn't have minded it at all, yet looking at the new additions, at the thin film of dust on the left side of the door grills, Shonali bit her bottom lip. She knocked hard against the cool steel.

From behind the door, she heard shouts and heavy steps. *Thump-Thump-Thump* against tiles.

A bright, fair face peeked out from the sliver of the open door before it was thrown wide.

Mrs. Gita Bharadwaj, if she had to guess.

Dressed in a saffron sari with green accents and an elaborate mangalsutra[1] swaying across her slender neck, the woman unlocked the outer door and beckoned Shonali inside. Clumsily stepping forward, Shonali nearly tripped and knocked over the small clay diya[2], the short stub of the wick still sopping wet with oil.

"Shonali, how good to finally meet you! What a surprise!" The woman threw her a dazzling white smile, lips painted a bright red. "Come in, come in. I'm afraid I've gained some weight. But I'll lose it again." The woman laughed loudly as if Shonali were a family friend. "Your brother told us all about you when we signed the agreement. How selfless to be taking care of your father."

Gita pulled a stunned Shonali into the hall and motioned for her to sit. "We have chai, tea, water...What would you like? I'll pour some Rooh Afza[3]."

"Nothing, nothing, please," Shonali said, her well-worn speech already cast aside. "I'm actually just stopping by to ask about the rent."

---

1. Mangalsutra - This is a necklace worn by married women across various communities in India.

2. Diya - A diya is a lamp. Usually it's a small, open oil lamp made of clay. You pour oil and add a wick in in the rounded area. These can be fancy or simple.

3. Rooh Afza - A common syrupy beverage, usually added to water or milk to give it flavor.

"Ah, I see." Gita's smile dimmed, but only briefly. She stood in the hall, in front of the kitchen door, hands barely crossed as if uncertain how to proceed. Licking her lips, she motioned for Shonali to sit once again on the divan, and she accepted the request.

"Aren't we paying on time?"

Gita's question failed to ring curious or even irritated. Rather, her tone was light and soft. And her eyes, so convincingly sharp and certain, peered down at Shonali as if instead asking, *Why would you ask us such a silly, troublesome thing?*

The woman scooped up a manila folder labeled with Padma 56 written in thick black Devanagari letters on the coffee table, fingering the papers on the side before placing it near a cabinet in the corner of the room.

"Well, that's just it. I haven't received payment in nearly three months, and I've tried to message you." Shonali played with the hem of her dupatta, looking away from Gita Bharadwaj.

The tenant straightened her shoulders and relaxed.

"How odd! What numbers do you have? Four months ago, we had to change ours," the woman began to prattle on. "Let me get you some tea. Don't get up. It's not a problem at all. What kind of host would I be if I let you sit there and starve, dear?"

Shonali nodded mildly, watching the woman turn on her heels, silver anklets clinking as her footsteps rammed into the tiles. Attempting to stop fidgeting with her scarf, she crossed her arms under her chest.

"And the payments?"

"I'm not sure, and I'll have to call the bank. But don't worry at all; we'll get it straightened out," said the woman. Then, a tiny click of her tongue as she returned from the kitchen. "Oh, I think Raj had some issues. He has a few investments in companies, and tax season is just starting. You know how these things go," Gita laughed and smoothed the sharp pleats of her sari. "But do tell me, beta, where are you staying?"

Shonali wanted to protest the informality. But it was a small battle. And she already felt a slight headache coming on.

"I'm not staying. I must be getting back soon," Shonali said flatly. "And, I'm sorry, is that the smell of gas? Is the cylinder leaking?"

The foul stench made her stomach knot. Fixing the piping would be another expense.

"Oh, yes, it's nothing, nothing at all. The cylinder is just running out, I'm sure," Mrs. Bharadwaj said as she returned to the room and slid open the window. "But you're going back so quickly? That won't do. Aren't you exhausted? Mumbai traffic is so tiring."

"I'm quite fine, Auntie," Shonali said. The terms of both respect and familiarity felt odd. Yet, she would rather use honey than vinegar to get her way. If the woman wanted to be chummy, Shonali could be chummy—so long as she left with a check or a bundle of cash. "I don't want to leave my father alone for so long. The maid will also want to return to her family."

"Of course, of course," Gita said, stroking her chin. "Why don't you stay with us tonight and return in the morning? Certainly, that would be better. And then we can get this whole mess sorted out."

The offer caught Shonali off-guard. She certainly was not going to stay in a one-bedroom apartment with two other strange men. Had the housewife completely lost the plot?

"No, I don't think that's appropriate."

"Oh, but you must! Besides, it is your flat." Gita grinned; her large mouth stretched wide from ear to ear. But her eyes held a cold heat, a tension that didn't quite match the friendly tenor of her voice or the white of her smile.

While Shonali knew everyone in the building, and it was technically her flat, the entire idea was more than uncomfortable. And the fact that her tenant considered her more of a guest than a disgruntled owner felt like a blow in itself.

None of this was going the way she'd planned.

A sense of dread swelled in her belly. She didn't even want to be here. She didn't even support the ideological arguments for renting. The entire concept was a racket. Everyone needed a place to live, but living as a renter was an existence dictated by the landlord's moral requirements.

When they moved to Pune, they had rented for years before her parents managed to pour all of their capital into their new two-bedroom flat. Years of penny-pinching landlords, society judgments, and reprimands for existing outside their tiny rented space.

Seeing Gita before her reminded Shonali of their last landlord. An older man, hardly a gentleman, always hovering, counting the rupees in rent, giving unsolicited advice to Shonali's father on her clothing, her school timings, and her mother's occasional kitty parties[4].

In the back of her head, a dull ache began to hum. Shonali curled her slender fingers over the hard cotton of her scarf.

"I'll think about it," Shonali said politely, standing. "Perhaps I will come back later when your husband is also home. There are still some people who I need to meet with..."

"Of course, of course." The host repeated a smile on her crimson-painted lips. "I'll be here."

Shonali felt Gita's shadow on her neck as she approached the door, a chill licking at her bones.

---

4. Kitty Party - This is a social group event for women. They may visit one another's homes or go to a restaurant or event. Everyone usually contributes some money towards each party.

THE ALMOST DEAD END

RUDHRANI

O NE COULD LOSE THEMSELVES in the vast topography of Mumbai—and that is what Rudhrani was afraid of. Already it had been two weeks since her new assignment, the missing person's case. Yet, despite her network of friends, acquaintances, and colleagues, only a fraction of the massive metropolis had been searched—with an emphasis on the nearby slums and gullies bordering Worli.

And to make matters worse, despite her uncle's proximity to the Mumbai Police Commissioner, there was little to support her search without a solid lead. Resources were spread too thin to spend on a Muslim woman from Worli, who the authorities believed might have decided to take a spontaneous vacation. The only consolation the Police Commissioner could afford was to send her the number of a junior officer at the local police station. Who, like his boss, only agreed to help once Rudhrani had a viable lead. Or if the daughter returned to officially file an FIR[1] —something that Asha couldn't possibly do.

The situation at Golden Deer Housing Society was worse. From the beginning of the case, any attempt to investigate the disappearance of Nazia Khan was thwarted. The day she arrived in Mumbai foreshadowed the challenges ahead.

Her flight ran over an hour late, the waterlogged streets transformed a half-hour cab right into nearly two hours, and when she reached the Eco Lodge, water submerged her ankles as she shuffled from the cab to the hotel door. It was the cheapest hotel she could find in the area, and it was also incredibly far from the housing society, near the southern edge of the district.

At first, it didn't seem much of a nuance, horrid weather aside. In fact, the next day the rains subsided into a casual drizzle. A simple introduction to the housing society and a review of Mrs. Khan's flat seemed to provide enough clues to get started. But that was hardly the case.

Rudhrani reflected on how optimistic she had been, almost on the brink of naivete. The watchman had been sitting at the gate in a damp plastic chair, his poncho shielding him better than the tattered umbrella overhead. She had smiled then.

"I'm here to see Nazia Kahn," Rudhrani stated.

He blinked his heavy eyes. "She's not here."

"When you think she'll be back?" Rudhrani pressed.

---

1. FIR - First Information Report, a document written up by police when a criminal offense is first reported.

"I'm not sure. She's gone to visit family, I was told." The man rubbed a hand on his knees as if warming them up.

"And who told you that?" Rudhrani asked.

"The committee manager, Mr. Kamble."

"I see. Well, I've spoken to her daughter, Asha Khan, who wanted me to check up on her. Wouldn't she know if her mother was visiting family?"

"I can't say to know what other people do," said the watchman. "I've never met the daughter. I've only been working here recently."

Rudhrani bit her lip. "May I at least see the flat?"

"I can't do that without permission from a relative," the man said, rubbing his forehead.

Suddenly, Rudhrani felt a jab in the middle of her back, her dupatta pulling against her neck. With a gasp, she looked back.

"Sorry, sorry beta," said a thin, older woman. In her firm hands were two heavy sacks of vegetables, the purple eggplants glistening through the plastic. "I lost my balance. It's so wet, you know. Are you looking for someone?"

Rudhrani nodded, taking a deep breath and adjusting her dupatta.

"I'm here to see Nazia Khan."

The woman stared at her blankly before her lips curved in a wide smile. "Oh, Mrs. Khan. She's visiting her family, I believe. Somewhere abroad, Dubai, maybe?"

Rudhrani raised her eyebrow and appraised the woman. Despite her politeness, something about the woman's stature unnerved her.

At the mention of Nazia's name, the stranger's eyes had sharpened, her pose straight and firm before her. Not defensive but assertive.

And what was there to be assertive about?

"I've heard differently from her daughter. She hasn't been able to reach her for a few days."

"Oh, well, you know," the woman shrugged, suddenly stepping back. "Perhaps Mrs. Khan didn't tell her. After all, what child leaves their aging parent alone in such a city? Perhaps if you leave your name and number, I'll call you when she returns."

Rudhrani eyed her suspiciously.

"My name is Amrita Sen," said Rudhrani with feigned confidence. Certainly, her cousin couldn't fault her for using her name. Just this once.

"Ah, Miss Sen. A Bengali, how nice. I'm Gita Bharadwaj," she said as she wrangled her phone from one of the produce bags. "And your number?"

"Why don't you give me yours, Auntie, and I'll call you later?"

Gita looked up at her, a dark shadow flickering over her eyes, before nodding. When Rudhrani pulled out her phone, the woman read off her number quickly.

"Aren't you going to ring me?"

"I'll do it later, Auntie. Your hands are full," Rudhrani said. "But thank you for your help."

At this, Gita appeared placated. Her shoulders relaxed even against the strain of the bags. "Do call me, beta. I can also let you know when the office manager will be here."

Rudhrani nodded, waiting for the woman to go. She watched as Gita walked slowly towards her building, not once looking back and then disappearing into a dim stairwell.

Perhaps she imagined the sliver of animosity. Regardless, she would not be calling her. Once she did, the woman would have her number. And with that, Gita could easily use an app to link her phone number to her real name.

The investigator turned back to the watchman.

"And there's no way I can visit?"

"No. As she said, Mrs. Khan is away."

"Just because Mrs. Bharadwaj believes Nazia Khan is away doesn't mean she actually is," replied Rudhrani, coughing slightly into her hand.

The man heaved an exasperated sigh.

"Look, what the residents say goes. If you can speak to Kamble then maybe I can let you in."

"And Asha's friend who came by earlier? Did she have to get the society manager's permission?"

The clouds above appeared coiled as rain-heavy strains began to churn. It wouldn't be long before another downpour started.

"No," he said. "But I didn't know that Mrs. Khan was gone then."

"And how did you find out?"

"Everyone seems to know," the man shrugged. "The next day, Mrs. Kabraji received a letter from Mrs. Khan saying she was visiting family. And she told me to tell that girl if she ever returned."

Rudhrani's lips pursed. A large droplet splattered against her ear. Glancing up at the sky, she pulled her dupatta over her head.

"And which flat does Mrs. Kabraji stay in?"

The man hummed. "I think, 301 of that building there," the watchman said, pointing at the left complex. "But she and her husband went out an hour ago. You may want to come back."

"And Kamble's number? "

The man nodded, listing the number effortlessly. Saving it, Rudhrani thanked the man and turned to look at the society one last time. What was once a quaint, almost romantic remnant of early Mumbai appeared drab. Windows that might have once been lined with basil plants or clotheslines remained dark and barren. But then, on the top floor of Mrs. Kabraji's building, the very same complex she knew that Nazia Khan lived in, Rudhrani noticed the glaring eyes of Gita Bharadwaj in the window.

Rudhrani attempted to reach Kaushik Kamble all day to no avail. Only in the evening did he finally respond to her call. But he refused to allow her entry on the premises, citing that residents were concerned about strangers lurking about.

"You can understand, can't you?" Kaushik's voice seemed to leer at her through the phone. "This society is mostly the elderly, living alone. They want to be safe."

Over the next few days, she attempted more creative approaches to gain entry, from asking residents who ventured outside to help her meet her "aunt" to trying to slip by when the watchman fell asleep.

Reasonably, the residents were on their guard. Mrs. Kabraji never made an appearance, either. And the strays, scenting Rudhrani as a new potential threat, barked whenever she approached the gate. Nothing seemed to work, no matter how hard she worked to enter the premises. Even with Asha on a video call with the watchman and Kaushik, they stood resolute against her.

And after five days, the society manager threatened to involve the police. Despite the fact she could probably talk her way out of a police confrontation or at least use her uncle's connections, any delay could significantly hinder her investigation. It wasn't a risk she was willing to take.

The only source Rudhrani could think of was the original woman who investigated the flat. Perhaps her intervention had spooked someone who knew the truth. Yet, Rudhrani had spoken to her early on and had nothing new to glean from questing her again. The young woman had visited under the pretense of a simple check-in and did not think to examine the scene for clues thoroughly. Nor did she confess to speaking to or noticing other residents.

At a loss with the society, she asked around shops and stalls Asha's mother might have frequented. There were a few names of family friends living across Mumbai—a few in Worli, but others in Juhu, Bandra, and Kurla[2]. Some had left Mumbai entirely. None had seen nor heard from Nazia Khan. Instead, they believed that she had

---

2. Juhu, Bandra, and Kurla - Like Worli, these are all localities of Mumbai.

traveled to London to visit Asha. To their minds, it was the only reasonable explanation for her prolonged silence.

Over the next two weeks, she worked with Asha to compile a list of potential sources while staying with her parents in Pune, a city only a few hours from Mumbai. Kaushik, at least, answered her inquiries about the other residents from Asha's list. Except for a handful of names, most had either moved away or died. The jittery manager, of course, did not know the current whereabouts of the living nor the causes of death for the rest.

And so, with a curated list of names and phone numbers, Rudhrani had gotten to work. For once, she was thrilled she had taken a full holiday from the clinic in New York rather than opting to work remotely from India. It took time, but without a lead for where Asha might be, locating the former residents was the best chance she had.

After what seemed like an endless carousel of calling housing brokers, potential friends and relatives, and the valid numbers Asha had given her, the sleuth had further narrowed the list of former residents to question. Hopefully, she could arrange the interviews quickly and pinpoint a tangible lead to Nazia Khan's whereabouts. She only hoped that Nazia was alive and merely lost.

But in her gut, Rudhrani knew that something malicious lurked in that tiny corner of this seaside luxury, something deadly.

And, sooner or later, she would find out what.

THE NEIGHBORS

SHONALI

T HE DOOR CLOSED BEHIND Shonali, the hinges groaning against the frame. Shuffling to slip on her shoes, this time she did trip over the diya in the corner, oil trickling on the cold concrete. Shonali clicked her tongue and crouched next to the little clay lamp, her fingers brushing up the mustard oil and wiping her hands on the soaked diya's edge.

Wiping her wet fingers on her dupatta, Shonali descended when she heard the dull thumping of footsteps on the terrace.

She remembered the repair work they had invested in the year before, just after the Bharadwajs had moved in, bolstered by sandbags and tarp to prevent leaks during the monsoon. Being on the top floor of an old, dilapidated building, their flat was particularly prone to water damage during heavy storms and occasional summer cyclones.

During her brief childhood stay in the flat, the water would seep through the false ceiling, streak stains dark and heavy, smelling of mold. The lights would flicker erratically, only to be replaced by candlelight. Her mother, small and fragile, would serve warm tur daal[1] and rice with fluffy soft roti, telling ghost stories from her youth in Kolkata.

After leaving the flat and renting it out, her father continued maintaining the terrace despite the several long rows he had about it with the society. Even with the good rapport she and her family had with the neighbors, the committee stated that as long as the leaks occurred within their flat, no society money would be spent on terrace repairs.

There was never enough money for the much-needed upkeep, especially as more and more of the long-term residents defaulted on their maintenance bills. Yet the maintenance and repair fund costs seemed to increase exponentially. And, of course, the leakage, once it infiltrated their flat, was the individual family's expense.

Shonali paused, listening for the heavy thuds above her. But she heard nothing—and no one entered the stairwell. Glancing at the closed door behind her and then at the threads of light at the base of the stairwell, Shonali decided to check up on it.

A stroll down memory lane couldn't hurt.

Her mother would take her there often. Shonali could remember the odor of dahi and sweet-smelling coconut oil Ma would rub into her scalp. Together, they'd sit on steel stools in the sun while the yogurt dried, each lock like a brittle twig. Ma would tell story after story to keep her occupied. In the faint drizzle of rain, Shonali could

---

1. Tur daal - Also written as "toor daal". This is a split pigeon pea dish.

hear the softness of her voice like a quiet song. Six years was too long to be without her.

Unlike her father's gradually declining health, her mother's cancer had, at least, been quick.

Today, the roof was empty, except for the line of tarp, sandbags, and an array of television and internet wiring strung up haphazardly across the battered and cracking cement walls.

Frowning, Shonali glanced around, looking for a sign of life. But there was only a cold wind blowing from the nearby sea. The absolute silence chilled her thoroughly—no birds, no cars, no chattering or sounds from nearby TVs playing too loud. Around her, skyrises loomed, but except for a woman in a yellow kurti sweeping nearly four more floors up in the building behind her, the vast complexes were deserted. It was like standing in a void; only the gray sky and the muted tree leaves pulsing in the wind kept her grounded.

Shivering from the cool breeze and the rain, Shonali decided to check on her neighbors. After all, she had to do something while waiting for Mr. Bharadwaj to return home.

No longer driven by anger or dismay, the trek down the stairs felt longer.

Shonali felt cold coiling in her stomach from the incessant quietness by the time she reached the fourth floor. Here, at least, so close to Nazia Khan's door, she should hear the echo of

Pakistani serials, ghazals[2], or even the afternoon adhan[3] —sounds she remembered so fondly from childhood.

Nazia had been a boisterous, friendly woman. Her kindness was contagious. And her daughter, Asha, had been Shonali's best friend during those years, so she knew the family's routine well enough. By this time in the day, Nazia Auntie would certainly be reclining on the couch, picking apart coriander leaves, eyes glued to a dramatic serial. While years had passed, one thing that had never changed, not once, had been the echoes of life resounding from the Khan household.

Shonali knocked. Once, twice, three times. Nothing.

Yet, as she was about to knock again, she felt the frigid chill of a stare on her back.

"The Khans aren't in. Haven't been for a while now," muttered a rasping voice from the bottom of the stairwell.

Shonali pivoted, startled, only to see another familiar face. Cyrus Kabraji, from the third floor.

But even the Parsi[4] man had changed drastically since she had last seen him.

Always a tall man, his figure now appeared short and gaunt beneath his regular dress shirt and pants, his cheeks sunken in. He leaned heavily on a cane, an overstuffed grocery bag in his trembling left hand.

---

2. Ghazals -A type of poem.

3. Adhan - The Muslim call to prayer.

4. Parsi - An ethnic group descended from Persian Zoroastrians.

"Kabraji Uncle. It's me, Shonali, from 501."

The clouds in the man's gaze evaporated slowly, and a weak smile stretched across his skull.

"Ah, Shonali beta. Su—no, Santosh's daughter. And what brings you here?"

"Just checking on the tenants. One second, I'll help you," she replied, skipping down the steps to carry the bag of potatoes and bottle gourd.

"Ah, that. Thank you," he said. "It's so dark in here now, I can't very well see where I'm going."

As he grumbled to himself, Shonali couldn't help but agree. The lights were hardly bright enough. She noticed that the lightbulbs were placed closer to the stairwell corridor, keeping the floors themselves dim. If the Khans or the Kabrajis hadn't had lanterns above their door, they would have been engulfed in total darkness.

Cyrus, with his shaking hands, searched for his keys in his pocket for a few minutes before finally opening the door.

"You could have called for me. I would have opened," Nina shouted from the hall, her voice less tender and more brittle than Shonali remembered.

Cyrus just hummed, removed his shoes, slipped on some house chappals[5], and took the sack into the kitchen. Kicking off her shoes at the door, Shonali entered.

---

5. Chappals - Leather sandals, although the term also refers to flip-flops.

Nina recognized her immediately, but Shonali could not reconcile this face with the voice. Nina had never been voluptuous, not like Pooja Desai, but she had certainly always looked healthy. Now she was as skeletal as Cyrus, her eyes tired, cheeks gray.

"Shonali beta, it's been so long! How are you? How are your parents? Why are you here?" Nina rattled off, engulfing her in a lukewarm hug. "Cyrus, come in here. One minute. I'll just bring some snacks. Sherbet? Chai? Sit, sit."

Shonali took her seat on the small, wooden-framed couch across from Cyrus. She didn't want to stay long. But perhaps she could get some answers. Since she arrived, the entire society seemed to be flipped upside down.

Even now, glancing around the hall, it was surprisingly sparse. Shonali recalled lavish bookshelves filled with thick tomes of classic fiction and mythology. She remembered knickknacks, gifts from friends abroad, and heirlooms, each one holding a small story. And Nina had told each story well.

Yet now the walls were barren, discolored lines the only sign of the heavy teak shelving having ever existed. The rich Persian carpet that had stretched across the tiles had vanished, leaving grayed, chipped tiles. What remained was covered in a thick layer of white dust.

Cyrus, his cane clicking against the limestone tile, came in and removed his house chappals near the sofa. The furniture was old when Shonali had last visited. Now it was practically ancient, and its age showed as the frail man sunk into the cushion.

"No bai[6] will come these days," Cyrus mumbled as he poked the coffee table with the cane.

"Why is that?"

Shonali could hardly believe that no one would come. After all, the rates in this area were likely fairly high. And the Cyrus family, in particular, were far more progressive, if she remembered correctly. They were hardly the type to haggle over ten- or twenty-rupee raises and often supported their maid and cook in whatever they asked. Her mother had stood in their doorway after a kitty party and reprimanded Nina for being too generous, Shonali recalled.

"They don't like it here. I can't blame them," the older man huffed, crossing his arms. "I suppose the committee will get a new service."

Shonali raised an eyebrow. If that happened, they'd raise the maintenance cost again. And the rent would barely break even. She resisted the urge to rub her forehead in frustration and pain as the low thrumming headache at the back of her neck reached her temples.

"It's cold," the older man grumbled again. "Could you please pass me that blanket?" He pointed to a basket at the end of the sofa.

Shonali almost jumped to it and pulled a thick, brown cotton blanket from the basket. From its folds, a thick cockroach crawled onto her kurti, its hard-wing shell as fat as her fist.

Squeaking, Shonali brushed it off, flailing her arms.

---

6. Bai - A term that means "woman" but is often used to refer to female domestic help.

The cockroach erratically fluttered its black wings, irate.

Quickly, she grabbed Cyrus's chappal and slammed it against the roach, grinding it into the floor. She breathed a sigh of relief.

But as she pulled the flip-flop away, nothing remained on the faux marble tile. Shonali looked on the underside of the chappal, but that, too, was clean. The roach had vanished.

"Beta, what are you doing over there?"

Shonali shot up, dropping the shoe.

"I was just getting this blanket for Uncle and thought I saw a roach."

"Oh no, I hope not. We just had a man come and spray the house. But they keep coming back. They've weakened the cleaning solution, I believe." Nina sighed. "And I don't know why you're getting so cold, dear. We should take you to a doctor."

"We went to my brother last week, and he said nothing's wrong," Cyrus said as he placed the covers over his leg. "Besides, I think those homeopathic pills from that Raj are working."

Taking her seat again, Shonali watched as Nina left a tray with rose sherbet and biscuits on the table.

"And what are you doing here again?"

"Just checking in with my tenants since my brother is away. After last time, we had some issues, you know."

"Oh yes, you rented to that business, didn't you?" Nina said, hands folded neatly in her lap.

"Yes. They had many issues placing their workers there. And then they stopped paying. It was a huge hassle to get them to move out."

"Well, they say you can only get your rent if you are there yourself or you do real estate full time. That's why we've never done it. But how lucky for you to have a second property."

It was hardly lucky. The flat had only caused her and her parents grief. And selling the damn thing seemed close to impossible. At least, that was what their broker had told her father and Ajit.

"Yes," Shonali agreed mildly. "And do you know them at all? The Bharadwajs?"

"No, not quite. They seem quite busy. Always coming and going. Always doing things. Honestly, I thought you had sold the flat to them. They seem involved with the committee."

"The committee? But tenants don't have rights in the committee, do they?" Shonali frowned, placing her teacup on the end table.

"Well, no. That's why I thought you had sold it to them. They know the remaining members of the committee well, it seems. They seem to get on well. Honestly, I was starting to regret that we didn't move into the Dadar Parsi Colony. We considered moving, but, well, it's hard to sell here." Nina sighed, her eyes misting with some distant longing.

"Who is still on the committee? I wasn't aware there was an election," Shonali said, feeling the headache threatening a full-scale migraine. There were only so many people in the society, so a new committee shouldn't be too much of a hassle. But, then again, with so much having changed, would she even be able to count on old ties if push came to shove with the Bharadwajs?

"Do we have to talk about this," asked Cyrus. "I'm only going to live so much longer, and the less we talk about this blasted society, the better." Shonali picked up her teacup and tried not to laugh. She felt the same way.

"Oh, don't make it a hue and cry about it. She's just curious," Nina laughed flatly. "A lot's happened, actually. And what they did to the walls. They could have at least put in a lift if they were going to do that!"

"Yes, I saw. It's quite dark now," Shonali mumbled, sipping on her lukewarm tea. Nina Auntie hadn't put any sugar or cardamom in it, but Shonali wasn't willing to ask for it. The bitterness pierced her tongue.

"It is! We used to have more stray dogs. More cats. The greenery feels a bit upturned now, also. Everything is changing. But I guess that's what happens when you get older," Nina sighed. "But where are you staying? Are you going back tonight?"

"I was planning to, yes. But I was going to visit Pooja Auntie and talk again with my tenants before leaving."

"Oh, you mustn't leave at night. I believe there's going to be a bad storm. Isn't there?"

Cyrus hummed in agreement, although it was clear he either didn't know or didn't care.

"One of my groups forwarded a weather report. We're supposed to get heavy rain tonight. At least stay until you can get something sorted. It's been so long since we've had guests."

"I thought you had kitty parties quite often, Auntie?" Shonali remembered her mother dressed up in a new sari, smiling on the staircase, the dusk light shifting through the lattice windows to create luminescent patterns on the glittering gold fabric.

"Oh, well. No one comes by anymore," Nina paused, pursing her lips. "I really can't understand it. It's like we're closed to the whole world."

"To make matters worse, she gets everything from that damned phone. And nothing is ever right," Cyrus chimed in, slowly leaning over to grab a biscuit. It crumbled at his fingertips.

"And the Nazia Khan? Uncle said he hadn't seen them…"

"It is strange. But you know, I spoke with Nazia a few months ago, and she mentioned going to visit Asha. She's in the UK, you know?"

"Yes, I remembered that," Shonali lied. She had no idea. They hadn't spoken since her mother died.

"Perhaps you could get in touch with her and just confirm. Their light is always on, but we haven't seen them. I received a letter from her saying she's in the UK with her. And why not? The summer here was terrible. Hotter than ever. And now this rain," Nina said enthusiastically.

"Could I see the letter?" Shonali asked timidly. Nina nodded, shuffled into one of the bedrooms, and returned with a simple envelope. It was addressed to Nina, but there was no address or mail stamp, as if someone had slipped it under her door.

Inside was a folded A4-sized piece of paper. And a brief message in Hindi saying that she was going to visit Asha and that she would be back in several months. There was no date.

Staring at the thick, uniformed Devanagari, Shonali felt off. Nazia's handwriting—and Asha's, too—had been softer, more fluid, hadn't it? But too much time had passed. Shonali folded the paper and carefully slid it back into the envelope. Time changed everything.

She thanked Nina and placed the letter aside. Her attention shifted to her former neighbor. While Nina had lost far too much weight, she hadn't lost her gift of gab and was quite content to rattle away, whether or not her guests were actively listening.

"Auntie, I think I'll go tell my driver of my plans and then speak with Pooja, if that's alright," Shonali eventually broke in. There was still a lot to get done. And she didn't want to impose further.

"Oh, that's fine, dear," Nina said as she picked up the tea tray for the kitchen. "Are you sure you don't need anything?"

Shonali smiled and shook her head before looking back at the blanket, dusty but hardly infiltrated by roaches. Exhaustion was setting in, and certainly, the cockroach had been a trick of the light. Or her nerves. It wouldn't have been the first time.

"No, I think I'll be fine."

THE STRANGE MAN

SHONALI

S HONALI WAS NOT FINE.

Since visiting the Bharadwajs, a headache had bloomed and now throbbed incessantly. The disappearing dead roach only exacerbated her anxiety. Was she going mad?

With the rain letting up, she considered booking a cheap motel or finding a snack shop to rest for a few hours. But there was a sinking feeling in her gut that she was stuck here for a while longer, perhaps another day or two. Shonali paced around the bottom of the society, weaving in between the buildings as she spoke with the maid caring for her father back in Pune.

"Of course, I'll stay," Toral promised in Marathi.

Shonali offered to pay her double for the late notice, hoping that the late bills would be taken care of and she would have the funds for it. But she still wasn't sure she'd have the money by the end of the day.

No matter how reasonable it sounded, Gita Bharadwaj's enthusiastic reassurances felt hollow. While Shonali was thankful that her society was more progressive in allowing tenants to have a say, there was something itching in the back of her mind—as if a significant concern had been misplaced. And as she continued to pace beneath the light drizzle, she tried to shake the feeling of dread from her bones.

At least Baba would be taken care of for the night. But now she needed to tell the driver. And her brother.

Siddharth was lounging inside the car, bare feet sticking out the window as he munched on a lukewarm bowl of chhola from their earlier pit stop.

"Siddharth-ji, I am going to be staying the day until tomorrow morning. Will you be available tomorrow?"

"It will cost extra," he said. But she had expected that, too.

"That's no problem. I'll pay you for the day and tomorrow's drive. Do you have somewhere to stay?"

"Yes," he said, pulling his feet back in. "Did you want to go somewhere?"

Her stomach grumbled. Shonali needed more than a cup of chai in her system. But she didn't have the energy to leave, she realized. It was better that she preserve her energy and save her limited rupees. Between the maid and the driver, her funds were running low enough as it was.

"No, not now. Probably not tonight. I'll just be in society. So, if you like, you can have the rest of the day off. I may call you in the evening to drive to a hotel. I'll send you the money now."

The driver nodded as Shonali tapped her phone app to send him the reserve funds. Once she showed him the successful transaction, he quickly left, and she was alone again.

Taking out her wallet, she had 2,500 rupees to her name. Enough for a night at a cheap hotel. With the additional driver payment, bank account funds plummeted below the meager minimum required to waive the fee. The rest would go to Toral mausi when she returned from Mumbai. Unless she could get Ajit to wire some last-minute cash or the Bharadwajs decided to pay up, she was stuck.

"Are you lost?" An unfamiliar voice, rich and deep, lulled her from money woes.

A tall, fair man in his mid-twenties loomed beside her, his large hands holding a portfolio case. He wore a simple knit T-shirt and jeans, his thick curls lightly brushed back with oil. He smiled politely at Shonali, dimples dipping into his cheeks.

"Not at all," Shonali said quietly. "And you are?"

"Arjun Bharadwaj, 501."

Ah, the son. Arjun was less of a boy than she imagined. Certainly not the "kid" her brother had referred to when providing details of their meeting. Easily twice her size, Arjun would have appeared formidable if it weren't for the calmness of his composure.

"Nice to meet you. I'm the owner, Shonali Chatterjee."

"Ma did say you stopped by today. I apologize for the inconvenience. I'm sure it'll all be patched up," Arjun said. "I hope this isn't taking too much of your time."

"Of course, of course, it's not a problem," Shonali said, wanting to clamp her teeth on her tongue instead. It was a problem. A big one. But politeness begets politeness.

"It's lovely here. I'm surprised you moved," Arjun commented, glancing around the society. "It needs some work, sure. But you're more likely to find older flats like these in Juhu."

"Yes, well, with my father's transfer to Pune and attending university, it became the most logical option," Shonali mumbled. "And you're from Mumbai?"

"Yes, I've mostly been raised here. But my parents were from Nasik and Pune. We've got quite a wide range, actually. My family tends to be more industrious, and I've got cousin-brothers all over. Certainly, it must be the same for you. Bengali, right?"

"I can imagine," Shonali said. "Yes, Bengalis. Originally from Kolkata, then Mumbai."

"And your family is big? Your brother was quite engaging to speak to."

"About average," Shonali said in an attempt to maintain distance, although the warmth of his words and tenor placed her at ease. "I'm afraid it's just us in Pune. My mother died six years ago. She had a sibling who died in childhood. And my father doesn't have family."

"Doesn't really?"

"We aren't close." Shonali sighed. In reality, her father did have family—two brothers. One was a volatile alcoholic, and the other had vanished long ago. Her father described the missing brother as a useless vagabond, and her mother claimed not to have known him. Shonali herself could not remember him, nor did she need to. Enduring her other uncle's drunken serenades and shouting matches were memories enough. Adding more dysfunction into the mix wasn't necessary.

"It's a bit old-fashioned this place, no lift," Arjun commented as if detecting her apprehension. "But well worth it. A real steal."

"I know. With the maintenance funds as high as they are, you would think they would install one," Shonali nodded in agreement. How he thought this place was a 'steal' was beyond her. True, the older architecture tended to incite nostalgia. But it was hardly livable compared to modern standards, especially for a family that seemed as affluent as the Bharadwajs.

"And Golden Deer? I guess it's better than some of these English names," her tenant replied, "I once lived in Sanctuary Heights, and it was so difficult to give directions. Sounds ridiculous."

"It really is!" Shonali chuckled. "I also prefer local and traditional names. Why we hang onto the English, I don't know. To be frank, I studied Hindi and Sanskrit literature at Pune University. English isn't my strong suit."

At this, Arjun raised an eyebrow. "What, no engineering or business? Isn't Pune great for IIT[1]?"

"To be honest, I wasn't up to it. There was so much stress, and with everyone being an engineer anyway, I thought I'd focus on literature and be a teacher," Shonali confessed, feeling more at ease. Something about him felt disarming. Perhaps it was how Arjun crossed his arms, listening to her story. She couldn't remember the last time someone had truly listened to her. "Honestly, I was very interested in Indian literature in Sanskrit, Hindi, and Bengali. I

---

1. IIT - Indian Institute of Technology. These are considered the top or premium universities in India.

spent a lot of time on my own studying retellings and variations of the epics. I don't often get to use it, but it's nice."

That was the truth, or the half-truth at least. She had taken the engineering exams, compelled to study to the point of sleep deprivation. When she wasn't pulling an all-nighter, nightmares jolted her awake in the early morning. Somehow, she had passed her exams, but just barely.

"What do you, then?" Arjun asked, shifting from foot to foot.

"Oh, I just work doing some editing for a new paper in Pune. It's alright. I'm trying to get into writing until I can get a teaching position," Shonali said, hoping a smile might add a pinch of hope to her voice and offset what she knew. Her job was going nowhere. But until her finances stabilized, she couldn't work outside the home and care for her father. "And you?"

"The family business," Arjun gestured to his briefcase. "Nothing too special. But I love the epics. They are so important but don't get nearly enough attention."

"I don't know if not getting enough attention is completely accurate," Shonali said, shrugging. At his silence, she glanced at Arjun. He appeared relaxed, still smiling, but his eyes cut deep at her anticipated disagreement, his shoulders squared.

"But I think you're right," she conceded, trying to size him up. This seemed to pacify him. In fact, he now appeared so relaxed, so like before, Shonali couldn't help but wonder if she had imagined the tension. "However, I have a more serious question: is there a cheap hotel around here? We can maybe discuss this more when I come back in the evening to meet with your father."

When Arjun leaned back, Shonali felt a gust of fresh air enter her lungs. As attractive as he was, his closeness was suffocating.

"Well, there's a good one down the road, maybe half a kilometer past the gate. New. We know the owners. Let them know I sent you, and they'll give you a good rate."

"Thank you so much," Shonali said with a strained smile.

"But you should probably head out before dark. There's been a strange man wandering about."

"A strange man?"

"Yeah. Slightly balding. Round face. Glasses. A birthmark on his right cheek. He just hangs around the gate," Arjun muttered. "I really don't know what we pay the watchman for. I think Pooja Auntie said he used to live here, or something like that, in our flat. Well, your flat."

Any hunger that had been lingering was gone as Shonali's stomach dropped. She felt her chest tighten at the mention of a birthmark that he claimed to live here.

It was her uncle, her father's brother. It had to be.

"Anyway, my father is likely going to come home late tonight. Come by tomorrow," Arjun smiled gently before leaving her alone.

She felt the chill in the air as it began to drizzle, slate gray clouds rolling over her head like a sheet. Crossing her arms, she began to head to the hotel Arjun suggested for some cover, at least.

If it was him, her uncle... good god! She hadn't seen him for years, over a decade, even. But she remembered her mother's sweet voice strained in anger, her father responding in kind. She remembered her uncle's name being bandied about, along with a few other epithets she wasn't eager to repeat.

Sujoy Chatterjee. What did he want?

THE FACADE

SHONALI

B Y THE TIME SHONALI arrived at the hotel, the rain had begun again. Eager for shelter, she barely glimpsed at the sign—The Prayag Hotel was sprawled with a neon yellow on white, in a Devanagari-styled English script.

An aged Maru-Gurjara[1] facade of inflexible marble gloomily prefaced the modern glass and metal above, a farce of polite architecture and historical chic, the dissonance made more apparent by the flat modern buildings surrounding it.

Inside was not much better.

The lobby was a cluttered collection of hard waiting room seats and artwork from across the country. Puppets, pottery, and supposed tribal paintings had been positioned without context, names, or descriptions. And while the works held her interest, they felt, as a whole, cacophonously clustered haphazardly beside

---

1. Maru-Gurjara - A style of temple architecture from Northern India.

one another, not because of their nature but because of their inconsistencies and inconsiderate placement.

The cultural heirlooms seemed like crudely scrawled signatures on a bar wall, without room to breathe, each piece demanding attention and receiving little notice. No matter how hard she tried to parse the items and see the uniqueness in their patterns, her eyes were interrupted by the next item, and the next, all the way to the lobby counter, which, highlighted with the same bright yellow as the sign, appeared as an eyesore. But at least it stuck out.

"Do you have a reservation, miss?" The man looked at her almost stoically, with a flint of disapproval in his eye.

"No," Shonali started. "Actually, Arjun Bharadwaj recommended—"

"Ah! Are you Ms. Shonali?" The man's eyes lightened; his eyebrows relaxed. "Yes, he just called a few minutes ago. We can give you a discounted rate. It'll only be two thousand rupees, plus GST."

Shonali ran the numbers in her head. Not that they were that complicated. Now that she had resolved to stay the night, she needed somewhere to rest. And this was better than calling the driver out again and spending hours in waterlogged Mumbai traffic. She could at least walk back to the housing society and cut transportation out of the equation completely.

Grudgingly, Shonali slid a single two-thousand rupee note across the counter, along with her identification card. The man glanced at it and shifted uncomfortably.

"Ma'am, it's another 360 rupees, the GST," the receptionist repeated.

Shonali ruffled through her bag for her purse again and pulled out her wallet. She was reluctant to part with her remaining cash. Not everyone accepted card or digital payments. And although her credit card was already at its limit, her debit card could cover the remainder.

Underneath the receptionist's judgmental gaze—or so she believed, too embarrassed to look him in the eyes—Shonali signed the paperwork, all the while feeling the cold eyes on the crown of her head. When she finished, she grabbed a few pamphlets of the city along with her card key.

Immediately after, a bellboy appeared. Shonali already felt the hole in her pocket but resisted the urge to wave him away. What good would another twenty rupees do her? She could only buy biscuits with that. And just because she was in a bad state didn't mean she could pass that off to others.

Following the hotel staff, she noticed foreigners leaving their rooms, smiling, swinging their umbrellas, and carrying cameras. NRIs[2] chatting in English with their children scurrying about, eager to jump into the indoor pool.

Yes, this was far above her salary range.

Room 807. High enough to see the sea, but unfortunately, positioned in the opposite direction, she saw another towering hotel from her cramped and locked window instead. She could only observe the building's vague outline as rain pelted against the glass.

---

2. NRI - Non-Resident Indian. This refers to Indian individuals who live abroad, typically for work or education.

Children giggling and racing past her room, feet thumping, muffled the monsoon patter and echoed even after the bell boy left her.

Sighing, she glanced at her phone and pulled up the hotel's description.

The Prayag Hotel was expensive—far more expensive than Shonali realized a hotel could be, even in Mumbai. Almost directly on the seafront and within view of the Worli Sea Link, the hotel's associates owned perhaps one of the most idyllic locations in the entire area.

Feeling guilty about Arjun's charity and enjoying the luxurious suite, Shonali sat on the bed and counted the meager amount in her wallet once more. *It was only for tonight*, she muttered to herself, *only for tonight*.

Removing her shoes and collapsing on the bed, Shonali sighed, closing her eyes. Beneath her lids, she saw Mrs. Bharadwaj's unnerving blood-red smile and glinting white teeth. Her amber eyes had greeted her with a knowing look, as if Gita Bharadwaj recognized Shonali immediately. And maybe she had. Maybe her brother had shown the woman her picture.

Grasping at her phone, she unlocked the screen.

The original residents of the Golden Deer had vanished. Even in her anxious state, Shonali had noticed the empty windows, the silent stairwells. Outside of the Kabrajis and Pooja Desai, the only person she might have known was Mrs. Khan. And she was, allegedly, on vacation.

But, even then, perhaps Nazia Khan or her daughter knew something.

Shonali knew she had Asha Khan's number tucked away somewhere. Even if the young woman was in the UK, she might have been there since before the tenants moved in.

She barely had to scroll down her contacts list to find Asha's number. Of course, it was possible the number didn't even work. The last time Shonali called was when she discovered her mother had cancer. True, their time together had been short. But a fierce kinship had formed between them in those early days—often in the courtyard under their mothers' gaze. And even with the distance between them, Shonali and Asha had at least informed each other of their successes. Occasionally, their sorrows.

Shonali bit the inside of her cheek. It had been six years since her mother died. It has been six years since she last called Asha. Would she even pick up the phone?

Her thumb hovered over Asha's name.

Did Nazia Khan know about Shonali's uncle? Given that he had once lived with her family in that flat, given his strong resemblance sans birthmark to Shonali's father, there was no doubt Nazia might have recognized him.

What was he doing here, and why was he showing up, *now* of all times?

Shonali only vaguely remembered the stout man with the round belly and the hairy birthmark on his right cheek. Her father's brother. In her youth, he had visited them often. But long before they left for Pune, the once cordial relationship between her uncle and her parents had begun to splinter. Fragments of her peripheral memory captured raging voices and half-empty whiskey glasses. Her mother's strained voice begged her brother-in-law to leave the house. And finally, silence, as her uncle's absence took root during family holidays like Diwali and Pohela Boishakh and Ganpati.

After all these years, what did he want with them?

Shonali's tongue grazed her teeth, and she clicked it against the roof of her mouth. She needed to work. She needed to call Toral and check on her father. She needed—

Shonali's stomach growled.

Grabbing a bottle of water from the adjacent nightstand, Shonali knew what she needed more than anything right now. Money.

And despite the lagging payments and her editor's strict instructions, writing an article was the best way to make more money quickly. Perhaps she could get something more than stress from this trip after all. Besides, she knew that she could use the distraction.

Using her phone, she began to type notes. Opening up the Mumbai tourist pamphlets, Shonali searched for ideas that she could pitch to her editor. Events. Museums. The best locations for Mumbai in the monsoon.

As if that hadn't been done before. But her boss kept her editing frivolous event pieces on mall-hosted fashion shows or pet competitions. Writing up such vapid magazine articles would have been more interesting than reading them and fixing grammar errors. However, the job worked with her erratic home-caring schedule, even if the payments were often past due. At least she had a job. Two years of unemployment and exhausting multi-round interviews was a trauma she did not want to revisit.

Slowly, as she searched for topics, she could hear her heartbeat in her neck, expanding towards her temples. A swelling sleep migraine.

Shonali tore open a snack bag and nibbled on the dried nuts—what she wouldn't do for some pav bhaji or vada pav. It was while she was imagining a plate of warm, fluffy bread street food that the noises began.

Thump. Thump. Thump.

She heard muffled sounds like someone moving furniture on the upper floor.

Shonali stood up and peeked out of the hotel room, rubbing her eyes. The corridor was quiet.

Between doors, there were plaques. She hadn't noticed them before, likely because the migraine was still pulsing behind her ears. Historical mementos, she realized, accented by photographs. Black and white photos of early freedom fighters and independence memorabilia. Stock photographs of Gandhi and his loom. The freedom fighter Subhas Chandra Bose shaking hands with Hitler.

But no source for the noise. In fact, the corridor maintained complete silence.

Sliding back inside the room, she turned off the light. Only rays of dusk, somehow cutting through the rain clouds, filtered into the room. Shonali continued attempting to work, shifting from brainstorming to correcting an article her editor had forwarded her in the morning.

Dusk turned into twilight. Shonali's eyes were dry and tired, but she needed this. She needed to do some work, if only for the sense of completion. And money. Shonali clung to the hope that she could turn this slowly spiraling disaster into something catastrophic.

But the pulsing headache gripped her skull. And the sound of thumping, running children continued—although whether it was from above her, below her, or outside her door, she couldn't tell.

Finally, when Shonali could take no more, she sent a list of article ideas to her editor in a sleepy stupor and dozed off.

THE SOLICITATION

RUDHRANI

RUDHRANI COUGHED INTO HER handkerchief. She had been driving all day, and despite the intermittent rains, there was enough dust and smog on the highways to exhaust her lungs. Perhaps it would have been more logical not to schedule four interviews on the same day. But she couldn't help herself.

The first had been over the phone and outside of the honking water tankers and shouts of the kacharawalla[1] outside her flat. She could make out most of the call. But immediately after, she had to drive to the far north of the city, to Pimpri. Then, to the far east in Kharadi, only to drive an hour back to the western neighborhood of Kondwa.

Varun Yadav, a retiree, was her last hope for a substantial lead.

The other four had largely irrelevant accounts because they left before Nazia Khan went missing. Two didn't know any tenants or

---

1. Kacharawallla - This is an individual who collects "rubbish", such as old pots, pans, technology, newspapers, etc. and resells them or gains money from collection.

residents Rudhrani had met except for the Kabrajis, Nazia Khan, and Chatterjee families, who hadn't lived there in years. She had a number for Shonali Chatterjee, but her call was always promptly ignored.

The only thing the three shared was the name of a real estate company—Padma Properties, Ltd.

Each of the former residents had been approached to sell their flats, and given the housing society's state of decay, they took what they considered a good deal and shifted to the neighboring city of Pune. It was not an uncommon story.

When she arrived at the housing complex in a residential gully of Kondwha, just off the main road, Rudhrani could see the shadow of a man waving at her through the iron-bared windows. And the man was there in the doorway to meet her upon exiting the lift.

"Would you like some coffee, chai?" Varun said quite amiably as he led her into the one-bedroom flat. The main hall was almost suffocatingly small due to the size and the amount of stuff the man had accumulated. But given his advanced age, no younger than seventy, there was no doubt that he still held a lifetime of cherished possessions.

"Water would be fine," Rudhrani said, coughing again.

He stopped and looked at her quizzingly.

"A cold? I'll make you chai."

"No, it's a condition. I simply cough a lot. No need to worry," replied the investigator. She didn't have the energy to explain cystic fibrosis at the moment. It wasn't a common disease, especially in India, where most who might be diagnosed with it died young.

"Nonsense," Varun replied as he hobbled into the kitchen. "I'll give you milk and turmeric, then. That's what my wife always gave to me and our son."

"And your son? Where is he now?" Rudhrani asked as she sat down. She heard the click of a lighter and the growl of the gas stove, but he didn't respond. Hard of hearing, too, she decided.

"I must admit, I felt very relieved when you called, Ms. Sen," yelled Varun from the kitchen. "I tried to explain the situation to my son in Australia, but he brushed me off. An old man like me says silly things, I suppose. Ah, I see I'm nearly out of turmeric. But don't worry, I have already started boiling water for the tea."

"Not at all," Rudhrani yelled back. She heard water gushing, and within a few moments, he returned with a glass of water. "What was the situation?"

"Well, it's an odd thing," Varun started as he sunk into a bright orange couch. "It all began a little over a year ago. A man from Padma Properties came to me with an offer to buy my flat. It was a low offer, and I tried to haggle. And why shouldn't I? The building may be crumbling, but I maintained my flat well. And it had two bedrooms! He seemed annoyed and said he would return with a counteroffer.

"Now, I knew he was going around to other flats. Mrs. Mistri told me quite a bit about it, how excited she was to move to Pune and be with her son, who was studying here. Then Balbir Singh, too, gave in and sold his flat. He was in quite dire financial straits, I believe. It's just a rumor, of course, but I believe he had a gambling problem...in any case, I knew that people were selling. But they wouldn't tell me the price, of course, and I didn't feel it right to ask directly. But I imagine they were getting offered around the same as I was.

"Now, about two months later, some new tenants moved in. It was common as there were a few houses on rent at the time. The Bharadwajs. I remember because they were so helpful," Varun paused, rubbing his chin. "In any case, they were a good family, the husband, and wife. And there was a son, too, I think.

"Normally, you know, tenants don't have the right to participate in the committee. But they made some donations and repaired the terraces. I was the treasurer at the time, and we really didn't have the funds for much repair. They were polite, good-natured. Most of us managing the co-op were old and tired of the whole thing. We appreciated their thoughtfulness. Gita and Raj both took leadership roles.

"However, a few months passed, and that damned real estate agent was pestering me all the more. Not just me but my neighbor, too, Ganesh Rao. A good man, a lawyer. We got along well. He did confess that he was getting frequent calls from different agents at the same real estate firm asking him to sell. Ganesh would never sell—his flat reminded him of his wife. There was one daughter, and she was married. He began to withdraw. We met sometimes and talked, watched cricket together, you know. Two widowers, what else is there to do? But he stopped coming by. He didn't want to leave his flat.

"Why did you think he stopped going out? Was he paranoid?"

"I would say so," Varun responded. "Thought someone was following him. Those real estate agents could get quite aggressive.

I felt off a few days, too, like someone was watching me. Especially on my evening walks. But he also was a fan of crime shows. I figured it must have gotten to him.

"In fact, he'd rarely even answer the door. I remember Pooja came over to give him some baingan bharta[2] she made. He barely opened his door to take it. And it took him quite a long time to open the door. Gita came, too, a week or so later, and he didn't even answer. I offered to take it and give it to him later. So, around tea time, I went and knocked. He answered, and I tried to give him the food. But he wouldn't take it.

"Then came the discussions in the committee. We had decided to hire a society manager to help us. He began making a public list of defaulters. Ganesh's name was on the list. I was shocked. And I told him so. I said, 'Kaushik, this is impossible. I know from my records that he has paid his maintenance fees consistently, without fail.'"

"And he replied that he only looked at the book of payments and had them written up on the computer. So I told him to look at the originals, and he said they had been accidentally thrown out. I was aghast. Then he responded that he entered much of the information himself and that it was in no way incorrect. But how can we check when we no longer have the original documents? At first, I thought it was just incompetence—"

The screech of a dying flame interrupted Varun. He jolted up and almost ran into the kitchen. The tea had no doubt boiled over.

---

2. Baingan Bharta - A mixed eggplant dish. Also a 10/10.

Rudhrani could hear him curse under his breath. When he returned, he offered her a half-cup of tea.

"Sorry, sorry. I lose focus. So, over the next few weeks, we ended up discussing the defaulter list. I noticed that the Bharadwajs were very enthusiastic about removing the defaulters, which I understand as we need money to maintain the society. But one has to live somewhere, don't they? And it wasn't long until Ganesh's name entered the discussion. Slowly, the remaining committee members began to agree. The remaining society members, too. As if their problems would be solved by removing our lifelong neighbor! Only Nazia Khan and I spoke out.

"So I pleaded with Ganesh from his door. I asked him to sell before they evicted him."

"I'm not sure what happened. But within a week, I noticed movers going in and out of his flat. I asked Pooja, who said she had signed off on his share certificate and allowed him to sell his flat. I was thankful at the time. I thought perhaps he had come to his senses.

"I decided to call him. No answer. For days, every time I called, there was nothing. I wished I had the number of his daughter. I knew she was in Mumbai but couldn't remember her address.

"But, and this is the terrible thing. His daughter Gauri called me nearly a few weeks after he left. She told me that Ganesh passed away the night before from a heart attack. I gave my condolences. And I mentioned that it was good he sold his flat to be with her in his final days. She didn't say anything for a long while. Then she told me he hadn't sold his flat at all. He had been kicked out!

"I, myself, was still getting the calls. And after that, I decided to sell. There was nothing left for me there. No true friends, no family. Nazia was still here, of course. And the Kabrajis. But the whole situation unnerved me."

"And the real estate agent, do you remember his name?"

"No, no," Varun said solemnly. "But I do remember my lawyer. It was the same lawyer the others had used to sell their flats. I'm not sure who recommended him first. He got me a few extra lakhs and charged a very affordable fee. Dilip Kapoor, his name was."

Rudhrani left Varun's tiny flat, her mind racing. She had, at least, a better picture of the inner workings of the housing complex. The major players. And a few names of those who might know more. The daughter, Gauri Rao, and the real estate lawyer Dilip Kapoor.

It wasn't much. But it was better than nothing.

THE TENANTS

SHONALI

SHONALI COULDN'T BREATHE, AND it was because something was wiggling inside her throat—she couldn't see, she couldn't move. All she could do was lie there, listening to the muffled sounds of the rain scratching in her ear drums.

Small, hard twigs lashed at her face. Her body was in agony, too; she could feel six thick sticks swimming against her soft inner flesh, tearing it at the seams.

She turned her head, and an oval shadow fell from her eyes. She could feel it coming up her throat, whatever it was, causing havoc in its path. Frantically, she tried to aid the creature, rubbing her throat erratically upward.

Finally, it crawled out of her lips, lazy and confident, drenched in blood. A thick, black cockroach, its massive size a testament to its age. It must have been nesting in her for years, waiting to come out.

She shrieked a silent scream as it extended its wings. And then—

Shonali was awake.

Morning hit her like a sledgehammer. While the migraine was gone, Shonali's body felt exhausted from the travel, the stress, and the damned cockroach nightmare.

Perhaps the vanishing roach itself stemmed from stress. She had always been frightened of them as a child, ever since they lived in Mumbai, where the humidity attracted roaches that grew with thick, heavy shells.

It started the summer her grandfather died, and her elder uncle went rogue. The flat had a strange and spontaneous insect infestation in the bedroom, causing the whole family to sleep in the hall. There were white, wiggling maggots that haunted her daily activities. She found them wiggling out from beneath the bedroom door. Shonali couldn't fall asleep as she thought of the thread-thin legs crawling over her flesh. The buzz of flies that hummed through the house didn't help either.

But the cockroaches raced up walls and profiliated in the kitchen and bathroom.

It was her mother who always calmed her down.

"Shonali," she would say, "don't you know how silly a roach is? They are always messing with themselves and running from us. Because to them, we are the dirty ones."

Yet, every time Shonali felt stressed, she'd begin to have a nightmare of those hot summer nights, of cockroaches crawling up her legs. Over time, that calming nature shifted. Instead, her mother pressed her more sternly: "Isn't it time you grew out of this!" Her mother's shrill voice still echoed in her eardrums.

Shonali shook away the exhaustion and the memories. She sat up and slowly began getting ready.

To her surprise, the breakfast was included in Arjun's bargain rate. Never one to waste, Shonali decided to eat her fill and forgo lunch. A greasy paratha, two eggs, fruit, three or four cups of tea. But the heavy meal only contributed to her sluggishness.

Wearing the same clothes as the day before, Shonali sighed and began walking to the flat. Again, she entered the perilous pathway, the surrounding buildings looming over her and over the old flat like judges. Again, in the sweltering rain, her soles still wet from the day before, Shonali trudged up the staircase, feeling a chill as she approached. The hallway lights blinked sporadically.

Knocking on the door, she met with Mrs. Bharadwaj's wide, scarlet smile. Today, the woman wore a light sun-yellow sari, her dupatta flat as cardboard over her shoulder as she welcomed Shonali into the house. There, she noticed Arjun and two men—one, with a thick mustache and round belly, was the father. Shonali recalled his face from the stamp duty documentation. But the bone-thin man with the gaunt, fair face beside him was all but a stranger.

"Welcome, welcome. I heard you stayed at our hotel. What did you think?"

"It was quite nice. I didn't realize it was your hotel—"

They owned the hotel? *That* fancy hotel? Despite the fact it had been Arjun's recommendation, despite his discount, a discount that now made more sense, there was a sense of violation as her stomach churned. Her wrists itched, and her blood ran still. Hot and cold and confused, it took everything she had to say nothing.

"Yes, yes," the woman interrupted, her fingers patting her mangalsutra. "It's not really solely ours. We just have a stake, don't let my husband fool you. This is my husband, Raj, and my cousin-brother, Dilip Kapoor. He's just here to chat before work, no worries."

"He's a lawyer," Arjun volunteered, smiling sheepishly. "Don't worry about him. It's all business-related things. He and father always talk after breakfast."

His mother shot him a cutting look, but the young man shrugged before pulling out his phone.

Meanwhile, Mr. Bharadwaj straightened his posture from the divan.

"Won't you get some tea for our guest?" he commanded softly.

"There's really no need—"

"Nonsense, nonsense. Come sit," he gestured to the chair beside his son. "You've come all the way from Pune by yourself. Of course, Mumbai is safe, but you must be tired."

Shonali awkwardly sat on the edge of the divan, trying as much as possible to keep herself small. Safe was a loaded term. Alone in an isolated society, far from home, with her uncle potentially stalking the gate, Shonali felt less secure.

"I'm just checking up on the rent. That's all. Because we have maintenance and other bills..."

"Of course, of course!"

Mrs. Bharadwaj came between them to set the tea on the coffee table, the demitasse gleaming white. "I've been telling her that it's a misunderstanding," the woman hummed, pushing an array of biscuits towards Shonali.

"It is. You know, with all the new tax laws—you know about the tax laws for businesses, don't you?" Mr. Bharadwaj said monotonously as he leaned back. He peered down at Shonali, and she had never felt as small as she did at this moment, although she could not explain why. Should she know about tax laws for businesses? Was he talking about GST?

"A bit—"

"Good. Well, we work in a few different industries. And we're being audited, so sometimes getting money from the bank is difficult. Nothing is wrong, of course, but the government needs to go through it. It's all about getting rid of black money. And that's important, you understand," Mr. Bharadwaj droned on.

Beside him, Dilip surveyed her motions with the greatest attention to detail. Under his gaze, Shonali resisted the urge to even shift her weight, although her foot had fallen asleep.

Shonali nodded hesitantly, holding the tea and saucer in her hand, but refrained from taking a sip.

"It'll only be a few more days."

"But it's already been three months," Shonali stumbled. "Is that a normal time?"

Mr. Bharadwaj was humorless, his round, hairy face long, his eyes filled with veiled irritation. "Well, you know how anything official is. It takes time. But don't worry, we'll pay your rent. We're good people, after all."

"Of course, I'm not doubting that—"

"Actually, we wanted to know a bit about you. Your brother mentioned you when he signed the lease," Mr. Bharadwaj interjected.

"Did he?" Shonali felt a migraine again, stemming from the strong odor of gas. "I'm sorry, is the gas on?"

"No, no. The cylinder is just finishing," Mrs. Bharadwaj said. "We had a man come out the other day. Nothing was wrong with the cylinder or the piping, he said. But as we were saying, you know, you're at a good age to be married. No doubt you'll be looking for a venue. Raj's family has some connections here and back home in UP[1]."

"I'm not really interested in marriage right now," Shonali said in a firm voice, one that was almost not her own, filtering into the conversation. "But I'd be happy to talk venues when that happens."

The woman pursed her lips, only for a moment, disdain flickering behind the normally warm eyes. And then, that look disappeared completely. Mrs. Bharadwaj clicked her tongue. "Of course, of course. I know it's hard to find a good match these days. But a good husband can take care of you. No more working or stressing about money; that's what I feel," she said.

Shonali felt as if her breakfast had turned into a boulder in her gut, and it weighed her stomach down to the tile floor. The pitter-patter of rain had turned into a full pelt against the glass, tree branches scratching and thumping at the window.

---

1. UP - A state in India, Uttar Pradesh. Capital is Lucknow.

"Is it not possible to get partial rent? It's been three months," Shonali said quietly, interrupting Mrs. Bharadwaj. She heard the woman huff.

"It would be impossible," said the lawyer gently. "At least today. But I believe I can speed up the process and get you some money in about five days."

"Uncle, I can certainly get something sooner than that," Shonali pushed, eagerness to leave driving her forward. "I have my father to take care of. And the maintenance bills here. I need something."

"Give us a bit more time," said Mr. Bharadwaj, his baritone voice heavy. "I'm sure this has been difficult. We know you are dealing with quite a bit at home. But we'll get you your rent, I swear it." He offered a large smile, his white teeth gleaming underneath his mustache, the canines unusually sharp.

Shonali glanced at Arjun but found him occupied by his smartphone, utterly uninterested in the topic at hand.

Mrs. Bharadwaj's irritation seemed to morph, briefly, into some kind of exaggerated empathy as she shifted next to Shonali and wrapped a fleshy arm around her shoulders, the rough edges of the cotton sari chafing against her skin.

"Poor girl. I know this is so difficult. Being alone. With your father the way he is. I know how you feel, really. Please, drink, drink," Mrs. Bharadwaj removed her arm and brought the tea closer to Shonali. She hadn't touched it.

"I'm really fine on my own," Shonali said, knowing she had already lost. She had been too soft, and to make matters worse, she felt confused. No doubt this family unnerved her. But she couldn't pin down exactly why.

"Of course you're not! You know, a girl like you, so dutiful, I'd have you married to Arjun immediately. Isn't that right, Arjun?"

She said it as if it would be a glorious honor, something that Shonali could only dream of.

Her son glanced away, either from irritation or embarrassment; Shonali couldn't tell. He remained utterly engulfed in his phone.

"That's... very kind of you to say. But I would really just like an answer on the rent. Today. I need to go back," Shonali pressed again.

"I'll see what I can do," Raj Bharadwaj sighed. "Let me call you tonight. But for now, we need to get on with business." He motioned to the lawyer, and together, the two went into the bedroom.

"Won't you stay for lunch—"

"No, I'm sorry, Auntie," Shonali said. "I promised to meet some other neighbors. But I'll call again in the evening."

"Of course," Mrs. Bharadwaj said, a thin, airless smile stretched across her lips. "Of course."

Outside the flat, Shonali found herself racing down the stairs, if only to be rid of the smell and the awkwardness of the entire conversation. Rage bubbled up in her chest, thinking of her brother telling these strangers things, being so open with them. And that righteous anger transferred to her phone.

"I can't believe you!" Shonali whispered a scream into her phone. "What did you tell them?"

"Tell who what?" her brother complained. "Do you know what time it is? I have work tomorrow..."

"The tenants. What did you tell them about me?"

"Nothing much. Just that you take care of Baba and work, that's all. What's that got to do with anything?"

Shonali's lips pursed. "Why would you tell strangers—people you are dealing with—anything about the family? Are you mad?"

"Why not, they're good people?"

"Good people! Good people who haven't paid rent in three months but own several businesses across the city, apparently. Yes, very good people," Shonali growled sarcastically. "Do you know how stressed I am?"

"Look, I'll send some money tomorrow. Don't worry. Have fun. You're in Mumbai!"

"Ajit—"

"Talk later, sis."

The click and the silence that followed drained her rage and transformed it into dread. She could feel it twisting like clay on a wheel, some unknown hand squeezing her earthen insides as they went round and round.

THE ESTRANGED UNCLE

SHONALI

A JIT WAS USELESS.

Shonali realized, amidst her exhaustion and fatigue, that she was entirely on her own. And perhaps she had been this entire time. Her brother had never been malicious, cruel, or strict, but his blatant disregard punctured whatever facade they had kept up between them. Theirs was a show of family but not of love. Of duty, but not devotion.

Ajit's dedication was as simple as accepting a string around his wrist. She was expected to give, and he to take. Promises of protection were meaningless.

Shonali wanted to weep.

But she didn't have the time. Or the energy.

Sitting in the stairwell, she watched the rain bleed into the open car park, inching closer to her each minute. The echo of rain might have calmed her on another day, but now it only drew out the rattle of exhaustion in her bones.

Wiping her eyes, Shonali tugged her phone out of her purse and texted Asha Khan. It was a quick, concise message. A polite back and forth-would be too awkward. Too unnecessary.

Without hesitation, she tapped send.

If she were doing this on her own, she would do it without much thought for the comfort of others. It was clear that the Bharadwaj family planned to draw this out as much as possible. Shonali would not sit back and let them manipulate her.

After scouring her email again for news from work, she stood up and stretched. She needed more information. And she knew who to ask: Pooja Desai.

As Shonali exited the staircase, well on her way to visit the Auntie in the second building, she saw a figure looming near the gate. And while the rain blurred his face, she recognized him immediately from his slouched stature.

Her uncle. Sujoy.

He stood beneath the narrow hut made for the watchman, consisting of a chair and a small table with a sign-in book. The guard was nowhere to be seen.

Sucking in a breath, she took out her umbrella and walked toward him, more water filling her faux-leather sandals, now peeling from age and rain.

He knew her, too, it seemed. They hadn't spoken since Shonali was a child, but she couldn't imagine she'd changed much.

"Shonali, Shonali, how big you've grown!" Her uncle's voice boomed through the deluge. He opened his arms wide for an embrace, only to slowly lower them again at her firm and closed stance.

"Uncle," her voice was cold. "It's good to see you. Why are you here?"

"I've been trying to reach your father. It's quite important. But I'm so glad—"

"Why?" she asked in a clipped tone. Cautious, unlike Ajit, when it came to sharing information. Did Ajit even know her uncle was surveying the property, a ghost sticking to the gate?

"It's a private matter. Between him and I, about the flat," her uncle nodded toward the building. At his sides, fingers fidgeted, digging into his pant pockets, sliding out again.

"He had a stroke and can't say or do much of anything, I'm afraid."

The news caught her uncle off-guard — she could see the shock behind his honey-colored eyes. He rubbed his bald head with a meaty hand, eyes gloomy and focused on her feet. Then, abruptly, he straightened his posture. Sujoy opened his mouth as if to say something but then went quiet. His gaze focused beyond Shonali. "Could you give me your number?"

It would be rude to reject her uncle's proposition. But she wasn't thrilled about him having her number either.

"Uncle, why don't you tell me yours, and I'll call you," responded Shonali. He paused before acquiescing.

He slowly recounted his phone number. Then, after Shonali slipped her phone into her purse, Sujoy grabbed her hands and held them tightly. They were sweaty, cold. Shonali resisted the urge to pull away.

"Shonali, call me. Please. Tonight."

Shonali glanced behind her to see what he saw. But there was only a thick blanket of rain.

He released her hands and bid his goodbye. She watched as he quickly slunk away toward the main road. Sujoy's eyes had been emotive, his fleshy hands almost pleading with hers. He was hardly the aggressive uncle she remembered, with whiskey on his breath, belting insults at her parents.

A gripping ache at her temples worked in tandem with the rain, a wet rhythm that seemed to keep her in a spiral. She felt like she was walking along the edge of an endless well, a circle of cold, slippery stone waiting to be shoved into a void. Shonali turned around again and glanced up. In the window of her flat, she could see a shadow behind the rain.

And then, suddenly, it was out of focus.

Her phone vibrated in her purse. Drawing it out and running toward a quieter staircase, Shonali's heart dropped.

The office. Her editor.

"Shonali. What is this email? I told you no more pitches until you finish the editing work I gave you."

"I turned that in two days ago, Sir..."

"And it was substandard. I read it. There were many issues. This won't cut it," he bit back. Of course, Shonali knew he wouldn't elaborate on her mistakes.

"Sir, you gave me two hours' notice for four articles."

"I don't want to hear it. This is a fast industry. You know this," her boss barked at the other end of the line.

Shonali bit her tongue. She had been with them since the promising journal was still around before it had been bought and reduced to a flimsy lifestyle rag. The restrictive tenor of the new administration was set to drive her mad, but she needed the work.

"Sir, I also haven't been paid—"

"Redo the article revisions, and then I'll check in with billing. And no more pitches. I know things were different when Mr. Deshpande was the editor, but we'll tell you what to edit and write about. Do you understand?"

"Yes, Sir," Shonali said, tears biting her eyes. "I'll get right on it."

At his angry click, Shonali gasped and wept—but only for a moment. Wiping the tears from her eyes, she sat on the stairs.

But there was something else.

Another message. This one from Asha:

"Hi, Shonali!

It's been so long! I've been trying to reach my mother for nearly a month now with no luck. I had a car accident here and was unable to travel and see for myself.

I've tried calling everyone in the society. I wasn't sure if you were still in Pune, and I figured it would be difficult for you to travel to Mumbai. But the society members either don't pick up, have moved, or say I'm rude for pestering them.

I've got an investigator on the case. If you know anything, talk to her. I gave her your number weeks ago. I've attached her number. Her name is Rudhrani Sen."

A Tight Spot

Shonali

JUST BEFORE REACHING THE hotel, a small cafe and bistro was nestled in the commercial section of an otherwise residential high-rise. Unlike the delectable and more affordable Irani chai stalls or namkeen stores, this European-style eatery served coffee and sandwiches.

Shonali sat in a booth. A cheap demitasse of espresso, all she could truly afford, steamed in front of her as she pondered her predicament.

The young woman switched between Asha's message and her call log. The caller she thought was spam had been an investigator all along. Guilt crawled into her chest. If she had known about Nazia's disappearance, she would have asked. She would have had the confidence to come to Mumbai sooner.

Her tenants were still a problem, too. In the case that the Bharadwajs, or even her uncle, turned to violence, she would have no support. Police would complicate matters, and her tenants appeared to have an extensive support network. In contrast, Shonali was isolated.

She brought the piping hot coffee to her lips and wrinkled her nose at the bitterness. The headache had begun to recede, but her eyes were still puffy and red from crying. Soon, she would need to call the investigator. Perhaps she could look into her own case pro bono since it may be related to Mrs. Khan's disappearance.

Taking another sip of her coffee, Shonali leaned back in the booth and watched the lightning as rain trickled down the window. Quietly, glancing around the nearly empty shop, she removed her feet from her sandals, cold air assaulting her toes.

Then, her phone rang. It was Toral mausi.

"Didi[1], I have to leave."

Shonali's voice tightened. "What?"

"I have a family emergency. My children are ill."

"My father can't take care of himself," Shonali said, scrambling. If this were any other time, if she were there herself, this wouldn't be an issue. She would have understood, would have taken care of her father alone, without complaint.

But this was the one time when she really needed someone in her corner.

"No worries, I'll send someone," Toral responded, her voice indifferent.

"Toral, I—"

---

1. Didi - Technically means "older sister." Often used by domestic help to respectfully refer to their female employers.

"I'm sorry, I have to go. I'll send someone else to check on him," Toral repeated, her voice breaking up over the phone before the line went dead.

Everything was collapsing. Her father's care, her work, her relationship with Ajit, and the blasted flat. Shonali placed the demitasse and saucer back on the stained table and ran a hand through her hair. She wanted to cry out, but she held the frustration close to her chest, locking it away.

Whatever budding nostalgia she felt toward that tiny flat earlier had dissolved, frustration and rage growing in its place. It was a sinking ship, and Shonali was tied to the bow. Going back empty-handed didn't feel like an option. But what was left? Her father was entirely paralyzed. He couldn't speak, eat, or move without assistance.

Frowning, she dialed for the driver. In all of her lethargy and rush to return to the flat, she had forgotten to call. The phone barely rang before the call failed. She tried again, to no avail.

"You look down." A fresh coffee cup was pushed her way—this one filled to the brim with milky-white coffee and a tomato sandwich on the side.

Shonali looked up, shaken to see Arjun Bharadwaj hovering over her. "I'm surprised to see you here. Isn't this a work day for you?"

The young man shrugged, running a hand through his hair. "I'm working from home today and just needed to take a walk. What about you? Want to talk about it?"

"Not really," Shonali said, attempting to temper the exhaustion in her voice.

He sat down across from her, regardless. "I'm sorry about my mother. She's a bit overwhelming at times. It's from a good place," he said, folding his hands on the table. "I just kind of tune some of it out."

"I'm sure she's all right. If there were different circumstances, I'm sure we'd get along fine. I just have a lot on my plate."

"Apparently." Arjun smiled innocently at her. His freshly ironed red shirt hardly wrinkled as he leaned his elbow on the table. "So, what's up?"

Shonali bit her lip. How could she tell him anything? For all she knew, he would go back and tell his mother. They would have more leverage than ever over her.

But who else did she have, really?

"My mausi just bailed on me. I have to arrange help for my father."

"Yes, your brother had said he's not well."

"Exactly," Shonali said, staring listlessly at her coffee cup.

"Well, you know, we have good friends in Pune. Almost like family," Arjun commented. "Since you are in this situation because of my father's bad luck, maybe we could help."

"I don't think that's appropriate..."

"It's just a thought," Arjun shrugged. "Let me know, and I can call them."

Shonali nodded and found herself taking his personal number down, primarily out of politeness. How could she lean on the same people who caused this mess?

Yet, Arjun was disarming, so unlike either of his parents—except in appearance—that he seemed almost unrelated to the whole affair.

And perhaps he was. After all, could all three of them, being as wealthy as they appeared, truly be living in that one small flat together? Or better yet, why would they even want to rent her shabby flat? Without a lift, decent parking, and leak protection during the monsoon? All the reasons her father and brother had been unable to sell the damn thing.

"How do you like the hotel?" Arjun asked, breaking Shonali's thoughts.

"It's very nice, thank you. But I've already checked out," said Shonali hastily. And a good thing, too. She doubted she would be able to afford another night, even at the discount rate.

"How come?" He furrowed his eyebrows in confusion. "They gave a good rate, right?"

"I just can't justify splurging like that," Shonali said. "But I really do appreciate the discount."

"Why don't you stay in your own flat until we get the money, then? Ma will cook for you."

"You can't be serious."

"I am," he said as he leaned back in his chair, arms crossed at the chest.

"You're suggesting I live with you and your family? You're strangers!"

"Not really," Arjun said. "We're renting from you; you have all our documentation in the rental agreement. That's hardly strangers."

"It's not exactly acquaintances, either. I don't think it would be comfortable for anyone," Shonali said. "And it would be stressful on your mother to take care of someone last minute."

"Not at all."

"I'll let you know," Shonali sighed. "But I should be able to get a room."

Arjun sat up, gulping the last of his coffee. Checking his phone, he stood, leaving his chair in the way. A waiter carrying a tray of mugs nearly tripped over it. Shonali offered an unheard apology as the man scampered away, her eyes on Arjun, who barely seemed to notice.

"Well, let me know. I've got to go now; work calls, you know." Arjun threw her another smile. "Just call me if you need anything."

She would be here another day—no doubt about it. Watching him leave, she decided to suck it up and begin arranging things. The sandwich and caffeine had certainly kicked in, and she needed all the help she could get.

Arranging a check-in for her father was at least easier than wrangling the rent money. Her college friends, at least those still in Pune, were too busy, but her neighbors, at least, agreed to help. They were home and said they would look in a few times a day. The elderly couple had retired, and the husband enjoyed speaking with her father before his stroke. And perhaps, Shonali thought, the good deed was a pleasant enough bragging right. Still, she knew she would need to offer them a gift for their efforts when she returned.

The next thing was finding a hotel close by to negate transportation costs. Her flat was too far from any public transit for it to be a feasible alternative. And even when rates weren't high, traffic would consume most of her day.

So, Shonali started with the nearest option—the Prayag Hotel. Even though it left a bad taste in her mouth to know she was funding the same people squatting in her flat. But to her dismay, the Prayag Hotel no longer had an opening. Hours passed as Shonali fruitlessly spoke to clerk after clerk.

Every hotel in the area was full or far too unaffordable to even consider.

THE SILENCE

SHONALI

S HONALI WAITED IN THE cold, hard coffee shop booth until the belting rain rested, settling on a firm but light patter on the drenched windows. It had taken two hours for the weather to shift, and she was certain the reprieve wouldn't last long.

With nowhere else to go and her driver refusing to answer his phone, Shonali decided to venture back towards the Golden Deer Housing Society. It was late afternoon bordering early evening, and she knew Pooja might be home and open to talking. As the co-op society's committee chair, Pooja would know anything and everything going on. Every flat's leaky faucet, every defaulter, every resident who spurned the maids and refused them pay.

The gully leading back to the flats was absolutely waterlogged, and any progress she had made in drying her shoes was utterly undone. But the sun, at least, peaked through thick rolling clouds that moved fast toward the Arabian Sea, even as it appeared that the star had been swept up by the tides, drowned and puckered.

Leaving her single bag near the stairwell of her building, Shonali decided to glance around the society first.

Despite Arjun's kind recommendation and his mother's superficially cordial disposition, Shonali felt, on the whole, unnerved by the entire situation. It had spun entirely out of her control. The more she seemed to grasp for something firm to hold on to, the more she realized the world around her was made of sand, always shifting around her.

She readjusted her dupatta over her shoulder. One side of the long scarf had been flirting with the muddy ground, a tinge of brown skirting the hem.

In her gut, Shonali knew that all of this kindness was a lie, figments of untruth hiding behind politeness. But more importantly, she knew that the Bharadwajs were up to something, that they had no intention of paying rent or even vacating. Due to her parents' own greed and oversight, she was completely and utterly stuck with the flat, which would leech more of her time and resources with every passing year.

And then, there was her uncle. Shonali had yet to muster the courage to call him. All she could remember was the last time he visited the Mumbai flat. During that time, she could only hear bits and pieces. Baba had been ferociously arguing with him in Bangla so that the neighbors might not understand their quarrel. Her uncle was spitting back just as many insults.

When Shonali had peeked outside the bedroom into the hall, she saw her mother leaning against the doorframe, a hand covering her tear-stained face, rubbing her forehead. She couldn't recall what they had been arguing about. The entire conversation had sounded like nonsense.

"You owe me, after everything I've done," her uncle had said. *"How can you be so cheap?"*

But her father had only stuttered additional insults. *"You drunken dog,"* he had said, voice raspy from the yelling match. *"I've given you enough, you weasel. Everything that goes to you comes from my children!"*

Her uncle had been an alcoholic, a gambler, and an embezzler. At least, that's what her mother had said later. Baba had refused to discuss anything at all. And just like that, Shonali found her family divorced from any other relatives. After her mother's death and her father's stroke, she only had Ajit.

But what could be said for Ajit now? How could her brother be so trusting of strangers and yet so distant from his own sister? Ajit had managed the property with his father, previously with the help of a broker. It would be his, after all.

But what was there really to inherit when it was common for tenants to refuse to pay for the final three or four months? The deposits couldn't even cover maintenance in case of default. And with the court process cumbersome and complex, the stamped lease documents proved to be useless. What could she realistically do? Pound her fist on the door of the Bharadwaj's primary residence?

So, she would eat the loss. But now her family couldn't afford to do that. Not with Shonali's meager pay and Ajit's unreliable wire transfers.

Shonali ran thin, brittle fingers through her black hair, massaging the scalp. At least, for now, her migraines had dwindled to a mild thrum.

"Are you alright, ma'am?"

Shonali turned to see the watchman. She had seen him standing beside Pooja Auntie when she arrived the day before. A good opportunity.

"I'm fine, I'm fine," Shonali said, shaking her head. "Um, could I ask you a question about Flat 501?"

At this, the man straightened. He nodded, albeit hesitantly.

"What are your thoughts about the current tenants? Do they seem all right?"

"I wouldn't know," the man bristled. "This whole society has problems."

"Does it?"

"Yes. Noises in the night. Gangsters and workers going in and out. Strangers at the gate, always. And the residents always want us to be alert. To stand when they pass. But it's a hassle even to fill a bottle of water...And it's just me now."

"Just you? For the whole society?"

It was only two buildings, true. And from what Shonali could see, the housing complex was mostly vacant. There were new name plaques, but outside of Pooja, Nazia Khan, and the Kabrajis, none of the original owners remained.

"The agency doesn't want to waste time on it. They don't even pay on time here..." The maintenance man turned away, massaging his eyes.

He was older, less than lean. Perhaps her father's age, or close to it. A paper-thin mustache peppered his upper lip, and he rubbed his hand hard against it.

"No salary. I've been here three months already..."

"That's horrible," Shonali said. What were her maintenance funds going to then, if not the staff?

"It's a bad place overall. Rotten people, it seems."

"Has it always been that way?"

"Only been here five months," the man shrugged. "The last guard here had a heart attack."

Shonali felt her blood chill from those words. Was that the watchman she had known? Or was it someone else entirely? Was it a natural heart attack or something else...?

"Thank you," Shonali found herself saying. "And your name?"

"Mohan Bagul."

Shonali nodded and offered him a twenty rupee note, which he slipped into his pocket. As he began to walk away, Mohan stopped and approached her, glancing around.

"About that flat, 501. They have people in and out all the time. They are very rude, the mother and son in particular. Very strict. Anything they don't like, they cause trouble. And another thing," the watchman said, his voice a whisper. "The husband has something for everyone."

"What do you mean," Shonali asked, furrowing her eyebrow. The tempered tone and ambiguity almost sounded like Raj Bharadwaj was a drug dealer. Maybe he was.

"I see him all the time, giving things to the few people here. If you're sick, he finds you medicine. If you need help with refurnishing, he finds you people. But soon, the people are gone." The man snapped his fingers. "Like that, I've seen flats vacated.

Some sold their flats. Some left on a stretcher. Some were kicked out. Then, strangers go in and out. And they tell me to let them in and to keep others out. Them and that lawyer of theirs."

He turned away to leave.

Frowning, Shonali looked at the other building opposite her own before glancing back at Mohan. She wanted to stop him, to ask him more questions. But his cautiousness told her to let it be for now.

Biting her lip, she decided to explore the entire complex.

Similar to her own building, the previous residents had packed up or appeared to do so. But there were far more vacancies. The rectangular outlines of old nameplates were traced in black, clean walls left behind where the plaques had been crudely removed. There were, perhaps, two new names out of the whole lot.

Making her way to the terrace, Shonali looked out upon the whole of the society. She couldn't help but notice the lack of vegetation or flowers. For the first time, she noticed the bald tree stumps, shrubbery, and malnourished hedges—a far cry from the thriving garden in her memories.

There had been bamboo and banyan trees—jasmine, palms, and other bright yellow and red flowers that her mother would pluck from the lower branches for her daily prayers.

Shonali crossed her arms and brushed her hair back.

How little this society matched her nostalgia. How cold it was now, fractured walls, sandbags, and naked branches. Organized, neat, but lacking in life.

It was how she imagined a cemetery. Not even the vibrant, albeit at times cacophonous, sounds of Mumbai penetrated the isolated garden. Not even the tiniest mumble or generator hum from the looming buildings surrounding them.

In the distance, Shonali heard the faint cawing of a crow. The longer she stood there, surveying the vast emptiness before her, the closer it became. Shrill, loud, and pulsing in her inner ear.

Feeling a sense of nausea overwhelm her, Shonali fished a bottle of water and her phone from her purse. She brushed the stray droplets from the screen.

Nothing.

No message from Asha. Or the private investigator. Or anyone else.

Here, in the ever-suffocating silence, Shonali felt tucked away from the rest of the world. She was entirely alone.

THE LAWYER

RUDHRANI

Despite leaving for Mumbai in the early morning hour of 5:00 a.m., Rudhrani still found herself in a cab stuck in a web of traffic at the border of Mumbai. But at least she had a plan.

Gauri Rao, now Gauri Bhave, had moved in with her in-laws and husband in Juhu, a beach-side, upscale district just north of Worli and the Golden Deer. Even better, a cursory search for Dilip Kapoor revealed him to be the owner of a real estate law firm aptly named Kapoor Associates, which was located in the nearby district of Andheri West. In other words, once she reached the western side of the city, she could ride south, down the Mumbai coast from Dilip Kapoor to Gauri and potentially to Shonali's flat. With an hour per trip, of course, between the waterlogged and congested streets.

Luckily, the law firm was easy to find. Settled into the front of a residential building, its only buffer from the torrent of rain a few shallow steps, the sign was impossible to miss. White cardboard with thick, square letters in all caps, shouting: KAPOOR ASSOCIATES, DILIP KAPOOR, LLB, REAL ESTATE, CIVIL, and CRIMINAL LAW.

Rudhrani raised an eyebrow. And it would be a rare breed or professional who had the time and resources to manage so many types of cases together, let alone able to run from court to court. On the firm's website, only Dilip Kapoor had been listed as the founder and primary advocate. But, certainly, there must be more junior lawyers at his disposal.

Yet, looking at what should have been a corner store or pharmacy, it was difficult to imagine a comprehensive legal team fitting into such a small space. Her suspicions were confirmed when she entered the building to find a waiting room filled with three chairs, a front desk with a young girl managing a phone, and a short hallway with two doors, one closed and the other slightly ajar.

Rudhrani approached the young woman, glancing at the haggard clients in the waiting room. All were well above their fifties, two men and one woman. One of the men slouched in his chair, rubbing the birthmark on his cheek, stared at her intently as if he found her familiar. Yet, for the life of her, Rudhrani couldn't place him.

But she wasn't here for a stranger. She was here to interrogate Dilip Kapoor—as subtly as possible.

The receptionist barely looked up from a notepad as she scribbled notes from the call. It was only after Rudhrani tapped forcefully on the counter that the young woman finally glanced at her.

"I'm sorry, ma'am. One moment, please," the young girl replied.

"I'm here to speak with Dilip Kapoor for an article I'm writing about successful lawyers in Mumbai for Lawteller magazine," said Rudhrani forcefully. If she waited until the receptionist was ready, she'd be waiting for at least another half-hour. The girl glared at her, putting her hand over the phone.

"I'm sorry, no media appearances."

"I'm sure your boss would beg to differ," Rudhrani replied. She had done her homework. This was one of the premier legal magazines in the country. And she had watched *Jolly LLB* and *Khosla Ka Ghosla* to enough times to probably wing it. Just barely. She was just asking questions, after all.

The receptionist opened her mouth to respond when a loud creak interrupted her. The door on the right side of the hallway, the one that stood agape, right behind the receptionist's desk, swung open. In its wake, a thin man stepped into view. Despite his frail frame, his presence seemed to take up the entire space of the door. He held his hands in front of him, staring intently at Rudhrani. And then he smiled.

"I apologize for your wait. My name is Dilip Kapoor," he said softly. "But she's quite right. We focus on work here, not fame or notoriety. And as you can see, we are quite busy." Kapoor motioned towards the waiting area. The man with the birthmark had mysteriously disappeared. "I just can't spare time to speak now. But perhaps if you arrange an appointment, we can speak next week?"

"I'm afraid I'm on a deadline. Today would be better."

Dilip frowned, his mouth stretching this already taut skin across his skull. "I'm sorry then, it's just not possible. But I can give you a quote. You said you're interviewing other lawyers, no? My key to success is focusing on the objective. Negotiating as much as possible to avoid the course. And, of course, the support of my family."

Rudhrani forced a smile. "That's quite good. But if I can extend my deadline, could I call you for a few more questions?"

"Yes, you can get the number online or from Divya when she's finished there. Now, Mrs. Bhatt, we have much to discuss," the lawyer said, turning his attention to the elderly woman in the waiting room. She blinked up at him and, leaning on her cane, rose to follow him into the office.

Rudhrani resisted the urge to click her tongue and looked back at Divya, the receptionist. The young woman ignored her, pivoting her chair towards the wall as she continued talking, this time on her cell phone. Rolling her eyes, she searched for the firm's number online and called it. But the phone didn't ring. So, she went to the firm's website she had bookmarked and tried the number there. Nothing. The investigator looked at the young woman expectantly.

"Excuse me, your number doesn't work. Could you write it for me?"

"We changed it last month," the girl said, rolling her eyes. She then ripped a paper off her notepad, scribbled a number, and handed Rudhrani the crumpled note.

She wanted to stomp out of the office, but she settled a huff and powerwalking into the street. And then Rudhrani almost bumped into a wall of wet cotton.

The man with the birthmark stood in front of the door at the edge of an awning.

"Excuse me, miss," said the man, his hands shooting to his chest as if surrendering. Rudhrani stopped to appraise him. "I've seen you before, at the Golden Deer Housing Society, no? I'm Sujoy Chatterjee."

Rudhrani blinked. She hadn't noticed him before, or at least not studied him intently during her investigation at the society itself. But she may have, in her peripheral vision, seen him in the walkway just outside the gate or even meandering down the main street. Still, his last name held her interest. The investigator has seen his surname on Asha's list of potential residents.

"Yes, I've visited there. And you? Do you live there?"

The man paused for a brief moment. "Technically, I own a flat. If you have the time, I'd like to tell you some information. For your article." His hands held each other, slipping slightly, and then he rubbed one sweaty palm on his pant leg. "It's very important. And a good story."

So, he had heard her ruse in the office.

"I noticed a vada pav stall further down. We'll chat there?"

Sujoy readily agreed. The ten-minute walk with him was a long, silent stretch of uncertainty. Over and over again, he would glance beyond his shoulders, his eyes scanning the street, the faces of the few passersby taking advantage of the lighter rain to grab groceries or snacks. Luckily, the small hole-in-a-wall restaurant was nearly empty, the vada pav fresh, the buns steaming. The investigator stared at him expectantly while the meal began to cool.

"You said you had a good story?"

Sujoy glanced around at the window behind him.

"Could we switch seats?" Sujoy fidgeted, the tips of his fingers tapping the table as he looked over his shoulder.

Rudhrani consented, and once the man had a clear view of the window, the tension eased from his shoulders, and he settled into a more lax state. Now, almost slouching, he leaned on the wobbling table, his hands folded in front of him.

"Dilip Kapoor is a crook. Perhaps the worst man I've ever dealt with. Let me tell you what has happened," he said, his voice but a whisper.

"Many years ago, my older brother robbed me of part of my inheritance. A flat in that very society. It has plagued many for many years that my brother betrayed me. Please understand. I'm not one for revenge. But one doesn't forget this kind of disrespect or selfishness.

"And I would have been content to let it lie if only to avoid seeing such a scoundrel. Yet, last year, I found myself unemployed. I had a wife to support. I needed money. Then, I thought of that house. Even if I could get a fraction of the rent, that would tide me over until I found work again. Of course, there was one problem. I didn't know where my my brother had gone to, what his number was, anything. For all I knew, he was gallivanting in Europe or America somewhere.

"That's when I decided to find help. I went to several lawyers who might be able to help me. Dilip Kapoor was one of them. And I found him quite personable, quite knowledgeable. I explained all about the flat. He, however, said that there would be little recourse in the courts at this time. That it would be costly and take years. He said he would investigate, and he did. I gave him the few papers I had, originals. Three months later, he called and said it would be best to wait until a better time. 'A better time for what?' I asked him. And he said to put pressure on my brother to sell.

"So I asked how long that would take. He said not to worry, and he gave me 20,000 rupees. I was thankful for that, of course. But I needed more. Everyone knows that Mumbai is expensive—even when sharing a flat, we pay at least 15,000 rupees!

"I decided to visit the housing society from time to time. To see if my brother would come. It wasn't long until new tenants had moved in. The young woman they rented to was gone, and a family was there. And at that point, the watchmen changed. I was told to leave the premises. To not come back. So, naturally, I went to Kapoor.

"But, of course, he did not help me. He said things would go at their own pace and would contact me if there were changes. I asked for my original paperwork back. He refused."

"And what do you think he is doing, Mr. Chatterjee?"

There was no doubt that Dilip Kapoor was an unsavory character. Yet, these few facts amounted to very little concrete evidence. Keeping paperwork? Paying a man money? A scam artist, most no doubt. But even if Sujoy was confessing the whole truth, there was little evidence to hold the lawyer on anything of substance.

"I believe he's taken my papers to use them to get the flat, destroy them, tamper with them, who knows. I believe he's cutting me out of the equation entirely," Sujoy said, his words blending into one another as his speech quickened. "He's a fraud of the highest order. An organized criminal, in my opinion. Who knows if Dilip Kapoor is his real name? And now he has people watching me. His own people are there, in that society."

Rudhrani frowned. The snack in front of her had gone completely cold as she listened to the conspiracy. It wasn't entirely impossible. But the connections were tenuous at best.

"You don't believe me," said Sujoy dejectedly.

"It's not that. I just need more." Rudhrani paused to scroll through the notes on her phone. She had Asha's list saved. "Are you related to Shonali Chatterjee, by any chance?"

He stilled before massaging his forehead with a heavy hand.

"She's my niece, my brother's daughter. I have tried to speak to her. But I doubt she trusts me. I'm sure her father has turned her against me," Sujoy said. "But that's why I'm talking to you. I have to make this right."

"Would it not be better to stress the importance to Shonali or your brother? It would affect them, too, no? Is it only Dilip Kapoor that has changed your mind?"

Sujoy looked at her, eyes wet. "No. You see, I'm not perfect. I do like alcohol a little too much. I always have. But...I will be honest with you. Until two months ago, I was okay to knock on Kapoor's door and ask for money. That's all I cared about. But now I'm dying. I've been diagnosed with late-stage stomach cancer. I've taken out loans for the chemo, but every day is worse than the one before it. I only want to reverse what damage I've done by getting this man involved."

Rudhrani leaned back in her chair and surveyed the broken man in front of her. She could see now that he was thin, far thinner than he should be. His skin was pale, his eyes fraught with sleeplessness. Yet this admission only steeped his story in more obfuscated waters. This could very well be a projection of his own inadequacy onto the lawyer—a desire to deflect and blame another party other than himself for his estrangement. All he really had was a frail conspiracy theory.

"And, if I may ask, what happened to cause a falling out between you and your brother?"

Sujoy's eyes hardened, and his arms crossed over his chest. "The past is the past. What is happening now isn't connected to our feud then. This is a whole other threat entirely."

"And the documents, what did you give him?"

"A will. Unprobated, unfortunately, from my father, signifying our inheritance to be shared equally. A share certificate with both our names," said Sujoy. "It's not much, but it's enough to contest with, I think."

Rudhrani didn't necessarily agree. She wasn't a lawyer, but she could imagine that anything unprobated could be dismissed by the court, especially if his brother could show more solid documentation or regular payments for the upkeep of the property.

"And is there anything else you can tell me? Anything at all that could prove your case or that I can use to investigate further?"

Sujoy looked at her listelessly, perhaps sensing her disbelief.

"I'm sure if you investigate into his firm further, you'll find something," he said. "He's a fraud, I'm sure of it. I can feel it in my bones. And it will affect my brother, too. And his children."

The desperation in his eyes perplexed her. Was it desperation for his relatives or for himself? Still, ignoring him could be a mistake, too.

She glanced at her watch.

"Look, Mr. Chatterjee. Why don't you give me your number? If I find anything, I'll phone you, okay?"

He nodded, quiet, and Rudhrani arranged from an Uber. Gauri was next, and she was running out of time. Stepping outside into the rain, she glanced one more time at the man behind the window, finding him with his head in his hands.

Gauri Bhave lived just a walk away from Juhu beach, and if they weren't in the middle of a monsoon, Rudhrani would be pacing on the edge of the waves with a roasted corn cob as she pondered the information from her encounter with Dilip and Sujoy. Instead, she was anxious about a potential flood and the hard wind shaking the palms outside of Gauri's window.

Gauri's husband was at work, her father-in-law was napping, and her mother-in-law was sitting in between Rudhrani and the young woman, her arthritis-riddled hands holding her cup of tea and saucer separately.

"What happened to Mr. Rao is so horrible. It was so sudden, him being kicked out like that, so of course we had to take him in," Mrs. Bhave said. "Family is so important, isn't it?"

Rudhrani nodded, holding the saucer carefully. Mimicking the mother-in-law, she poured the tea into it and then sipped at the rim, which seemed to please the older woman.

"My father was sick," Gauri said slowly. "He wasn't well. We did what we could for him. But, of course, it wasn't enough. I tried to get a clear understanding from the committee, but they had the records that he hadn't paid. And the amount with interest was so high. There wasn't anything we could do."

"We did all we could for him," Mrs. Bhave interjected. "A man by himself, these things are likely to happen. Especially in old age."

"Did he mention any problems he had with the other society members? Tenants? Or solicitors wanting to buy his flat?"

"He was anxious. Very paranoid. I was worried about him, but I was never able to visit. We have four children, you know." Rudhrani could guess how busy she was, but Gauri's eyes glanced to her mother-in-law. No doubt she was taking care of more than just the children.

"When he moved in, was anything odd?"

"No, only that his health had taken a turn for the worse. He had become pale and thin; he couldn't eat much without becoming sick. He had these lesions, too, on his arms," Gauri said, motioning to her forearm. Her mother-in-law shook her head. "He had medicine, but it didn't seem to help."

"Did you get it checked when he died?"

"It was heart failure, so no. He died at home, and we cremated him soon after. But I think we still have the bottle. Let me see," Gauri said as she left and promptly returned. "It's an ayurvedic medicine for blood pressure. It has ashwagandha and a few other things. Nothing you couldn't find in a pharmacy. My good friend is a doctor and said nothing in this would cause a heart attack."

Rudhrani took the bottle and rolled it in her hand. The labeling was a well-known brand. She glanced inside to see a few green pills.

"Did you try these?"

"Yes, my husband did. But it didn't seem to agree with him. It made him nauseous," said Mrs. Bhave. "Honestly, all medicine makes me sick. I prefer to avoid it whenever possible."

"And, if you don't mind me asking, do you know the name Dilip Kapoor?"

Gauri frowned and looked up as if pondering the question intently. "The name sounds familiar. I think, perhaps, his name was on some paperwork when they kicked my father out."

She got up again and returned, her hands clutching a stack of papers—notices of expulsion, eviction. Rudhrani thumbed through them. Dilip Kapoor's signature was scribbled at the bottom of the pages.

"Can I take these and make copies? And could I keep these pills for the time being? I'll return them by the end of the week."

"Yes, of course. There's a stationary shop just down the road," Gauri said. "And there's no need to return the pills. We won't be using them."

Rudhrani left, carefully folding the papers and keeping them in her purse. The day was hardly over, and she had much left to do.

The Emergency

Shonali

AFTER TRYING ONCE AGAIN to secure a room at an affordable hotel and failing, Shonali called Arjun. While she wouldn't be staying the night, she opted to stay for dinner. She couldn't afford to return home without something to show for her efforts. Even a meager payment would be a win.

So, with a brief WhatsApp call with Asha and the society's watchman, Shonali managed to convince the society manager, Mr. Kaushik Kamble, to allow her to stay in the Khan's flat overnight. She was a flat-owner herself, and her connection to Asha made it hard for the man to refuse Shonali. The man had agreed to stop by the society with an exasperated sigh. Rubbing his wire gray hair, he glared at Shonali as he handed over the extra pair of keys to the flat.

"If you knew you were coming beforehand, you should have organized this properly," Kaushik admonished as he straightened the cream collar of his dress shirt and adjusted his watch strap. "It's quite rude and pushy."

"I know, I'm sorry," Shonali had apologized sincerely. She hadn't meant to inconvenience anyone. "I hadn't meant to stay this long."

He clucked his tongue against his teeth, but she could practically hear the criticism rattling from his deep-set eyes and clenched jaw.

"I help run about ten societies. I'm not some message boy. Dealing with complaints about waterlogging, squatters, lawsuits, share certificates..." Kaushik grumbled. "I don't even get conveyance pay."

Shonali paused. She didn't have enough to offer him. Not now, when she had no idea how much time wrangling her rent would take.

The older man dislodged the awkward pause by dropping the key into her hand. Shonali thanked him, but he only shook his head in response, his eyes glaring down at her.

No matter how brief the transaction was, it was humiliating. Shonali hated that she was showing herself in such a weak state that she was now dependent on a myriad of faint acquaintances, on strangers.

Her only relief was that the Khan's flat matched her memory, except for the excess dust that lined every surface. Nothing had been touched or thrown out at first glance, although the wooden teak furniture's chipped face revealed age and wear. No sign of struggle. Besides the nearly empty fridge—only a few condiments and a rotting piece of cauliflower had remained—the entire flat appeared to be normal as if Mrs. Khan might stroll inside within the very minute.

But the supreme quietness made her disappearance all the more unnerving. Where could she be? Did something happen while she was out?

Shonali felt her mind race as her fingers traced books on the crowded shelves. She had loved this bookshelf as a child for its polish and deep dark hues. And the thick, leather-bound book spines had enticed her just as much. Above it sat a mat and inverter hooked up to the switchboard.

Between her mother, Nina Kabraji, and Nazia Khan, it was no surprise she had pursued literature. What Shonali learned from stories in those few formative years in Mumbai had given her a source of respite from their crowded flat, a deep pleasure in the power of words and stories.

There was, of course, normally an ornate Quran nestled near numerous volumes of Urdu ghazals, history, economics, and world literature. Mr. Khan had been a professor if she remembered correctly. In what, Shonali couldn't say.

But she noticed that the holy book was altogether missing, although none of the other volumes had been touched. A clue, perhaps, or a red herring. After all, Mrs. Khan might have taken her Quran with her when she went out. Unlikely, but possible.

On the coffee table lay a couple of second-hand paperbacks of true crime thrillers, the name *Nazia Khan* marked in curled English cursive and Urdu on the title page.

After surveying the flat, Shonali sat on the couch, leaning back into the cushions. The pillow covers had been stripped off; a clean lemon scent clung to the cushions.

Sighing, Shonali realized that there wouldn't be much to do before she met with her tenants once again. So, she began to work. Reviewing articles, proofreading them, and offering suggestions.

They were dull, but that dullness unfurled the tension in her mind, so much so that she lost track of the time. Dusk died down and made way for the evening rain, the ambient noise kilometers away as she tapped away.

It was only when the door creaked open that Shonali looked away.

Arjun stood there in the doorway, his tall form careening forward in the darkness, eyes bright. Had he always been that tall?

Her stomach dropped. Hadn't she closed the door? Or had Shonali, in her anxiety, failed to notice it was slightly ajar?

"Didn't realize you were staying down here."

"I'm a good friend of the Khans," she replied, although her statement sounded more like a question. Asha *did* give her permission. But it was more out of duress than anything else.

"Are you now?" Arjun smiled, staying at the door frame. "We're veg only, I'm afraid."

She tilted her head at him. *What an odd thing to say.*

"That's fine. I am, too."

"Good," he said. His eyes roamed over her face, intimately scanning her. At that moment, a frigid air gripped her. He appeared to be an entirely different person than he had been in the morning.

"Should I come up?"

"We're going to have dinner in a few, so yeah," Arjun nodded. "And you're sure this family is okay with you staying here?"

"Yes. As I said, we're friends," Shonali repeated.

"Well, come up in a few minutes then. Maa doesn't like waiting around," Arjun said, his voice quiet, before slinking out the door in the stairwell.

Shonali watched where he had been, apprehension rising. This was it—she was going to get something, anything, out of them. Glancing back at her phone, she quickly finished the remaining article and sent her boss a message before grabbing a dupatta from her purse.

It was too late to back out. And it would be rude not to show up.

Shonali wanted to smack herself. Should she really feel guilty about potential breaches of politeness? These people were lying to her. But it wasn't like she had any option. And it was better to placate them.

After all, the Bharadwaj family appeared to be much larger than her immediate tenants. Arjun and his parents seemed to have an extensive network of powerful family and friends, but Shonali knew she was on her own. Estranged from her extended family, far away from home, with a bedridden father and a brother thousands of kilometers away, she couldn't afford to make enemies. Not yet. Not now.

Taking a breath, Shonali went up to the flat.

It was dark. Behind her, the fluorescent light flickered erratically. As the door opened, the light went out, shrouding Mrs. Bharadwaj's round face in the darkness. Shonali could only see the red of her mouth as she cursed under her breath and the twinkling gold at the shell of her ear. A cold, clammy hand grabbed her wrist and yanked Shonali into the house.

"It'll be on again in a minute. Come sit," Mrs. Bharadwaj said, pushing her forward.

Shonali heard the purr of an inverter. Then the room became dimly lit, the brightness in flux. The window was ajar, and the fan churned air on its highest level. Arjun and his father were on the floor near the table, steel thalis in front of their hands, already shredding hard roti.

Mrs. Bharadwaj brought her in and directed her to sit across from Arjun while the woman herself promptly sat between her husband and Shonali.

The thali was almost overflowing with rice and buttered roti. There was okra, kidney beans, bitter gourd, and curd. The merging aromas made her mouth water in anticipation. Did they eat like this every night? Or was this just because she was a guest?

"Eat, eat," Mrs. Bharadwaj egged her on before stuffing a roti full of sopping red kidney beans between her lips.

"Yes, we're so happy you could join us," her husband said, albeit with a flat undertone. "We really love this flat. It's so close to other businesses, so quaint. And don't worry, I spoke to the bank. They'll be unfreezing the accounts soon. So, you'll have your rent."

"Oh, let's not talk business so much," Mrs. Bharadwaj said.

"She wants to know about the state of things," her husband grumbled, his mouth full of okra. "I'm just clearing the air for a pleasant evening."

"Apparently, Shonali's staying with the Khans just below," Arjun interjected, his eyes sharp as he looked directly at Shonali.

"Oh, really? Isn't it a bit dirty? I doubt anyone has cleaned," said Mrs. Bharadwaj as she scrunched up her nose.

"Not at all," Shonali replied sharply. "The Khans are very clean. Haven't you met them? Nazia can barely stand the sight of dirt on the bottom of her chappals."

Thinking back on it, she was surprised at how clean the apartment was. Considering that Nazia had been missing for over a month, the flat really should have been in a worse state.

"Oh yes," the mother shrugged. "I suppose I saw the woman. Impossible to tell, though, with the burka and all."

"It's not a burka; it's a niqab," Shonali said softly. "We'll all have to meet and have tea one day."

Mrs. Bharadwaj snorted at this, and her husband threw his wife a cutting look.

"Anyway, it's good to hear about the bank troubles resolving. I'm sure that is a relief for your business as well," Shonali said, switching the subject.

She couldn't afford enemies. Not on her own. Not with them so close.

"Yes, we're quite busy, you know. Arjun is, too, as he'll inherit the business. Only son, you know."

"That's good," Shonali said mildly. The okra tasted like ash on her tongue, and the kidney beans tasted like iron and raw chili powder. The smell had been deceiving.

Mrs. Bharadwaj opened her wide mouth as if to comment on their good fortune when a shaky yell burst in the hall. A frantic knocking followed.

It was Mrs. Kabraji.

Mrs. Bharadwaj wiped her hand on a nearby towel and opened the door, flecks of daal residue on her cheek.

"Help, please. Cyrus took his medicine, and now, I think he's having a heart attack. I can't understand this phone. It keeps asking me to push numbers, and I can't follow. I can't get a person. Can you call the ambulance?"

The lights flickered off again. Shonali watched the bulking shadows rise, the men's silhouettes blocking light from the window, eyes bright in the darkness.

And the lights flickered on again.

Mrs. Kabraji leaned against the door frame. Never before had she looked so small, so frail, as if she might break at the lightest of touches. She wept, hands rubbing her eyes, phone in a trembling hand.

Mrs. Bharadwaj sped past her, followed by Arjun.

Shonali felt herself grasping for her phone, calling the emergency number with the ease and familiarity of a full-time caregiver.

The entire evening went in a flash. Shonali comforted Mrs. Kabraji along with Gita Bharadwaj. The two sat on either side, stroking the woman's back. Shonali then found herself in the kitchen, rummaging through drawers to make tea as they waited, hands trembling, a light odor of gas seeping in.

The ambulance eventually came, carried in the stretcher, taking up the whole narrow staircase. The Bharadwaj men went with Cyrus as he was carried away, helping Mrs. Kabraji into the ambulance and following her to the hospital in their own SUV.

Shonali watched from the bottom of the stairs while the rain puddled in her bare feet. It had turned heavy again.

"Come on, we'll get you some chappals," Mrs. Bharadwaj said, the warm and soothing voice she had used with Mrs. Kabraji suddenly cold.

The entire stairwell was flickering into darkness—until the power burst with a loud crack.

Shonali kept her phone torch on, keeping track of Mrs. Bharadwaj in the darkness, who suddenly seemed to be larger than she appeared in the light, her face marred with shadows. Eyes cut back across her like glass as the woman brought Shonali into the house and dug chappals out of a cupboard near the door.

"What a night," the woman muttered to herself.

Food laid out on the table, half-eaten. The woman's jaw strained, the flecks on her cheek dried and black.

"That's the thing about growing a family," her voice was unexpectedly light and cheery. "You'll understand when you're married. You always have someone at your back. Of course, we all have our roles to play. Help me here."

Numbly, Shonali began helping Mrs. Bharadwaj with the dishes.

"I'm looking for Arjun, you know," the woman said, thrusting her chin out quite proudly. "Of course, there are love marriages, which is fine. But he's so picky, too. And really, you never know about these girls until you check them out. I'm sure you understand. You're from a proper family."

Shonali stayed quiet, letting the woman prattle on. The adrenaline was pumping through her veins, a mild ache in her temples. Her feet were chilled to the bone.

"And you'll need to find a good man at some point. Of course, I can see you and Arjun together. You two have quite a lot in common. But you really need to use more cream," said the woman, briefly stroking Shonali's arm. "Certainly, you can be lighter."

"I'm afraid I don't know him well enough," Shonali restored, eager to free herself from this woman.

"Ah, well, get to know him while you're here. You can't take care of your father forever. Your brother can handle that."

"My brother is out of the country."

"Exactly. Let him hire a maid. You need to think about yourself. About being taken care of. Take my advice, and find a good man quickly. An upstanding one who protects how things should be," she almost muttered to herself in the darkness. Her painted red nails scratched against the metal plates as she washed.

"And I need a good, dutiful bahu who understands family in this house. Such a sad state I'm in, can't you see?"

The woman smiled at her, but the smile was bitter and cold, and the only thing Shonali could think of was to escape her presence.

"Do you not have family in Mumbai, Auntie?"

"Oh, we have family everywhere," she grinned at Shonali. "Of course, I grew up in UP. In a small flat, similar to this one, in fact. Three sisters and a brother."

"That must have been fun, having such a big family," Shonali said. But the woman merely shrugged as if disinterested. "Where did you stay before our flat?" Shonali pressed delicately. "It's so small for three people. I was surprised when you decided to rent."

The older woman clicked her tongue, closing the small window over the sink. "Oh, you know, money is the main criteria these days. It's always important to save."

"I was thinking the same," Shonali said, the tenor in her voice more open. "I was thinking of selling for the same reason."

"Oh, you don't want to do that," Gita said. Shonali could feel the woman's eyes size her up. And, suddenly, she felt small. "A place like this? It's so old, you won't be able to sell it for under two crores. But no one will give that amount. Not for a one BHK[1]. Not for a single BHK with so few documents—it's so old, after all. You'll end up paying a fortune in discounts and taxes. Trust me, dear, selling is far too difficult to do alone."

As the adrenaline drained from her blood, the pregnant silence strained the air between them, each waiting for the other to speak first. Shonali felt sleep weigh on her mind, the scent of gas still aggravating her headache. She needed rest.

Yet, something about Gita Bharadwaj's rant rankled her beyond her crude comment about her skin color. Something she couldn't fathom. Certainly, the flat was old. And given the time period, documentation would have been sparse. But that was hardly an issue, right? Her father wouldn't have held onto a flat without their name on it for so long—not when her mother was convinced he could sell it. She had tried, several times, to pressure him into selling before her death.

But he had wanted to wait.

"It'll be worth more later," her father had grumbled. "Let me take care of it."

But now the money for repairs, finding a buyer, the decayed state of the entire society—the value was only in decline.

Shonali helped as much as she could in cleaning up the kitchen and living room before politely leaving, much to Mrs. Bharadwaj's displeasure. Shonali could tell her mood by the woman's pursed lips and irritated eyes, even in candlelight. And the flat's prospects continued to harangue her, even as she tried to push the thought away.

Slowly, Shonali said goodbye and made her way downstairs to the flat, closing the door as she heard heavy footsteps on the stairs and low, booming male voices. Arjun and his father, no doubt.

Slinking inside, Shonali wanted to curl up in a ball and sleep. Collapsing onto the couch, she pulled out her phone.

"Ajit, it's Shonali."

"Yeah, yeah, I'm getting ready for work. What's up?"

"Mr. Kabraji had a heart attack."

"Poor man. Is that all?"

"Is that all? Is that all you can say? The man taught you how to play cricket."

"Eh, well, just because his son was there. These people tend to keep to themselves, anyway."

"Ajit, they were our neighbors, our friends," Shonali sighed, rubbing her forehead. How could he be so callous?

"Look, is there a point to this call?"

"Okay, yes. You said you'd send money. I haven't received a text about a transfer."

"Jeez, am I a bank now?"

"It's not that! But I'm living in Khan's flat while I try to get rent so I can run the household and take care of our father. There's barely anything left."

"Are you that irresponsible? Don't you have a job?"

"They're late on paying again," Shonali mumbled. She should have saved this conversation for her morning. But most likely, he wouldn't be in the mood to send anything late at night his time.

"Look, just go home then. I'm sure they'll pay," he muttered. The irritation in his voice almost scalded her.

"Oh, please! I think the mother is more interested in my marriage than paying rent."

"Oh really?" her brother's voice lightened. "Maybe she's got a point?"

"Are you serious?"

"Well, you aren't getting any younger."

Shonali's lips formed a firm line, rage ballooning in her throat.

"You know what, I shouldn't have called. And you know what else? I'm selling the flat once they leave."

"Shonali—"

"Don't. I'm sick of handling things for everyone else. I'm getting rid of it. I'll put it in an emergency sale. I don't care if I get two rupees for it, especially since our uncle keeps showing up," Shonali muttered, ready to hang up. Let her brother stew over that for an entire day or two.

"What?" An edge cut into his voice. "What do you mean he's showing up?"

"I didn't talk to him. But he just hangs out at the gate."

"He's a liar, you know. And he probably wants the flat."

"But it's in our name, isn't it?"

His pause startled her. Shonali held her breath, her heart skipping a beat.

"It's in our name, isn't it?" she repeated cautiously.

"Not exactly," her brother sighed. "It's in both father's and his name, officially. He 'sold' us his portion unofficially."

Shonali's back straightened. "So, what does that mean? How do you sell property shares unofficially?"

Did her father really just take some money and skip getting the paperwork signed and stamped?

"Just don't talk to him. Don't say anything. He might want his portion of the flat," her brother said. With the tenor of his voice, she could imagine him hunched over the side of his bed, biting his thumb's nail anxiously.

"We can't afford that. What if he asks for some of the previous rent money or something like that?"

"I doubt he will." For the first time since they were children, her older brother's voice sounded small, minuscule, uncertain. "Just don't interact with him, okay?"

Shonali agreed and clicked the phone off, feeling the blood drain from her face.

That flat. She hated it. She hated it more than she had hated anything in her life. Its entire existence smacked of a hollow status symbol, a burden, a black hole, a cursed inheritance, a cosmic joke. It was an anchor tied around her foot, effectively keeping her father's ego satiated and her underwater.

Exhaustion took over. She still tasted the ash in her mouth from Gita's tea. Leaning back into the deep cushions, Shonali eventually drifted into slumber.

THE INVESTIGATOR

SHONALI

OVERSLEEPING WASN'T A REGULAR habit for Shonali. In fact, in most cases, she woke before sunrise, even if she had fallen asleep in the early morning. But today, she found her eyes cracking open at close to ten in the morning, her body sore, cold, and aching. Her bones creaked as she stretched on the couch. She rubbed the sleep from her eyes, attempting to scrub away the fatigue.

Even though cockroaches did not plague her dreams this time, Shonali felt dirty. She had worn the same clothes for three days, her sandals still soggy.

Yawning, Shonali stood up, her phone smacking the tiled floor. She cursed. Wiping the screen with her thumb, she noticed a WhatsApp message from the investigator's number, sent only a few minutes ago. She accepted the request, and Rudhrani's text appeared.

Call me.

Sighing, she tapped the number and went to the kitchen to search for tea leaves. The phone rang twice.

"Rudhrani Sen? This is Shonali. I just got your message."

"I'm glad I finally got through to you. Where are you? In India, I take it?"

"Pune, normally. But I'm in Mumbai now," she said, scratching her itching ankle with her foot. "Are you also in Mumbai? Asha said she hired you to look for her mother."

"Yes, I am. You own a flat in her society, don't you?"

Unlike Shonali, the investigator's voice was alert, awake. Shonali found herself self-conscious, realizing that her words might still be slurred from fatigue.

"We do. It's in my father's name. I'm looking after it. Not very well, though. Have you found Nazia Khan yet?"

"No, but I was hoping to speak with you," the investigator said. Then, there was a brief pause. "I wanted to know if you were in contact with her or if you could get me in the flat."

"You haven't been able to investigate?"

"I tried to get access to the property for more searching, but Kaushik thwarted me at every turn. He threatened to call the police. But since you are a flat owner, I figured you might have a way in. Or you could get in yourself and tell me what looks different."

"I'm actually here now," Shonali said. "I stayed here last night."

"Seriously?" There was a tinge of excitement in Rudhrani's voice. "How was it when you entered? What does it look like now? Anything odd? Missing?"

"It's a bit dusty but not nearly as bad as it should be. Moldy and rotten cauliflower in the fridge. Pillow covers and a Quran were missing. But everything else was normal. What is the reason they wouldn't let you in? I just had to show a video call with Asha."

"Because I'm not a resident, they were suspicious, even with Asha's approval. I figure someone is hiding something. Have you heard anything since you've been there?"

Shonali poured herself a glass of water. "Mrs. Kabraji, whose flat is just below Nazia's, said she received a letter saying Mrs. Khan went on vacation."

"Did she show it to you?"

"She did. It did feel off. The handwriting didn't look right, but I had figured so much time had passed..." Shonali said and took a sip of water, soothing her parched throat. "Unfortunately, her husband was taken to the hospital last night, and she's likely with him. It may be hard to get in and find it for ourselves without her permission."

"And, Shonali...are you noticing anything else? Any odd figures or coincidences?"

Shonali paused. Everything was turned upside down. Anxiety bubbled up in her chest at the idea of telling the woman from the beginning all that had happened. And, yet, with a childhood friend's mother missing, she couldn't afford to be secretive, either.

"Shonali, are you still there?"

The young woman blinked, her fingers tapping on the countertop. "Yes, I guess. I doubt it's too connected. Most of the residents have moved out, and few have moved in to replace them. My tenants are essentially squatting. And their idea of hospitality...seems almost malicious. I can't describe it properly. But it's unusual."

"And their names?"

Shonali listed them off.

"Does the name Dilip Kapoor mean anything to you?"

"I think so," pondered Shonali. She took the glass of water back to the couch and sat down. "If I remember correctly, Gita Bharadwaj said her cousin's name was Dilip Kapoor. Is that important?"

"It might be," the woman responded. If she was asking about it, it was likely that he was significant. Just as she was about to speak again, a loud cough jarred Shonali from her place on the couch.

Instead, she put the mobile phone on speaker and placed it away from her on the table while waiting for Rudhrani's cough to subside.

"Are you okay?"

"Yeah, don't worry about it. It's a long story," the investigator said, taking a deep breath. "Do you have any family that knows about what's going on?"

Shonali's stomach twisted like a snake, so tight she was almost in pain. How much could she trust this woman with? But at the end of the day, Shonali knew she had no one else. She took a deep breath.

"I have an uncle. We aren't on talking terms. I've seen him here, around the society."

"And did he talk with your tenants? Or anyone else?"

"Do you think he's involved in this?" Shonali crossed her arms tightly around herself.

"I'm looking at it from all angles," Rudhrani sighed. "I'm waiting to make some copies, and I have another potential lead to follow up with. Will you keep your phone on or let me know if you notice something else odd? I'll do the same, of course."

Shonali agreed readily. She needed help, especially with this new information.

Rudhrani then hung up, leaving her alone once again.

How did her uncle fit into all this? And why would the building manager prevent Rudhrani from entering the flat, even with Asha's approval?

She pulled herself off the couch and dragged her aching limbs to the kitchen. After several minutes, she managed to discover a packet of tea leaves and a half-empty container of powdered milk.

As Shonali went to turn on the red gas cylinder, she stopped and decided to lift it. With Nazia being officially missing, everything was circumspect. The weight of the cylinder wouldn't tell her much. But it could tell her something—how much it had been used.

Despite her threadbare muscles, Shonali lifted the hefty gas cylinder almost effortlessly. It was nearly empty.

Yet, the room didn't smell like gas. Reviewing the bright orange pipe that led from the stove to the top of the gas, a leak looked unlikely. Then she reached for the nozzle, its black switch upturned. It was on.

Shonali froze.

Had she turned it on, or had it been on when she entered the flat?

Carefully, she recounted her movements the night before and this morning. She hadn't made anything in the kitchen the night before. Nor had she gone to turn off the cylinder out of habit. The thought hadn't even entered her mind. And even this morning, the first time she had approached it was moments ago.

No, she hadn't turned it on.

That meant two things. Either Nazia failed to turn off her near-empty cylinder before leaving, which was unlikely. Anyone using this style of gas would be well-accustomed to turning it off when leaving the house or sleeping—a safety measure to prevent potential combustion.

But if she hadn't left it on, did she disappear from the flat itself?

Her eyes shifted back to the pillows, bare of their casings and smell of lemon soap.

Of course, there was a third option. That someone had been inside the flat and was using the cylinder itself.

Forgetting the prospect of tea, Shonali began to shuffle through the cabinets and papers. Pulling out books, documents, and photo albums, she made her way to the bedroom. Eventually, she stumbled onto a little red booklet tucked in a plastic bag inside the bedside drawer.

Every gas cylinder replacement will be logged in this little guide. She thumbed through the lined pages quickly until she found the last entry.

The last delivery had been made just over three weeks ago.

These cylinders often lasted one to two months. It shouldn't be empty now, especially given Nazia had been missing for the same amount of it.

The revelations chilled her, and Shonali quickly typed up a message to Rudhrani. Then, after sitting on the bed for a few more moments, she garnered enough energy to return to the kitchen.

Shonali put the tea on and walked around the flat, investigating once again. Looking for anything that could be useful. Something about her uncle, the Bharadwajs, the other residents, or even Dilip Kapoor.

But her amateur sleuthing turned up nothing of interest.

Pouring her tea into a washing demitasse, she sighed and sat by the window, looking out on the sterile grounds. She noticed a small crowd near the gate. The rain had just barely started.

The watchman, Mohan, was there. And Arjun, as well as a few other strangers from the society. Standing up, she tried to see if she could tell what was going on, but to no avail. Quietly, she slipped on her chappals and went down. Cautiously, she approached the crowd and peered over their heads.

Laying spread on the ground was her uncle, barely dry blood around his head like a halo. A police officer stood beside the body, writing in a notepad, clicking his tongue to the roof of his mouth. He glanced at Shonali before growling at the crowd to move away. He was speaking back and forth with the watchman.

Shonali turned away; her face was ashen.

Her uncle lay there, dead.

Looking up, she noticed Arjun giving her a piercing stare.

"You heard the man," he said quietly to the residents. "Let's all give the police some time to work." He motioned for onlookers to leave.

The police officer must have noticed Shonali's pale face and stricken demeanor as his gaze focused on her. "Did you know him?" He demanded more than he asked, his meaty hand resting on his belt.

"There's no way she could have known him," Arjun said lightly. "She's our landlord and just came for a visit. But we've seen him drunk around the gate before. Usually, he wanders off on his own."

Shonali frowned, the lies sinking into her gut. Of course, she didn't know him, at least not well. Not anymore. But he was her uncle. Could she let Arjun lie for her like this, primarily when so many people within the society would have known him? Would you have seen him? Pooja Desai, the Kabrajis, and even Nazia Khan would have remembered him, even if he lived here well over a decade ago.

The police officer's eyes narrowed, watching her, then looking back at Arjun before waving her away, too.

THE ESCALATION

SHONALI

S HONALI PACED IN THE corner of the car park. The morning shower had escalated into a full-blown storm in minutes. A harsh, cutting wind flew water in all directions.

This had to end.

With her uncle's suspicious death, Shonali knew that she could become a suspect in the investigation. She had been alone all night and in the morning. She had just spoken to him the day before. If what her brother said was true, she'd have a motive, in a sense, to kill her uncle—to keep him quiet and not share the profits from the house.

A bitter groan passed her lips.

Profits! She wanted to laugh.

Instead, she was left with a bundle of stress. Everything felt wrong, hateful.

No, she needed to leave. She needed her payment.

Biting her lip, Shonali climbed the stairs of the flat resolutely, her pulse beating in her ears. Her bony knuckles rapt at the door with abandon.

"Mrs. Bharadwaj," Shonali's voice was strained. It didn't altogether sound like her.

The door opened almost immediately. Wearing a thick cotton sari with bloody red embroidery, Mrs. Bharadwaj's eyes were black with kajal and sharp.

"Mrs. Bharadwaj, I'm planning to go back tonight. But I really need a firm date for the repayment as some token of confidence."

"Oh dear, did what happened downstairs scare you? It's quite frightening."

"It's really nothing to do with that," Shonali said slowly, careful that her voice didn't waver.

The older woman looked at her, eyes piercing into her own like needles, almost knowingly. "Tell me, did you know that man?"

Shonali pursed her lips.

"He looked like a degenerate. Probably killed by another drunk." Mrs. Bharadwaj chuckled to herself. "These types are all the same, you know."

"Mrs. Bharadwaj, I'll be by tonight. I need something, even a check I can cash later this week. So please relay that to your husband."

"We'll do that," Arjun's baritone voice responded from the divan. Cold, yet firm. Shonali looked his way and nodded as if in thanks. But he, too, stared at her with mild irritation.

"Thank you. I'll be back around five."

"My husband returns at about six. It's better to come then."

Pausing, Shonali glanced at their faces once more. Calm, collected. Sated, almost. She nodded again, thanked them, and left the flat.

Taking a gulp of wet, humid air, Shonali rubbed her brow and began her trek down. She needed to talk to someone, anyone. And calm down.

Her phone vibrated in her pocket. Glancing at the caller ID, she wanted to shrink away into nothingness. Her boss.

"Shonali, what is this?"

"Sir?"

"You've only sent me two assignments. Where is the rest?"

"I'm getting them to you today, sir. There was some complication with my internet, and a relative had a heart attack," she said. It was close enough to the truth.

She heard a click of the tongue on the other line and then a sigh.

"Look, Shonali. If you can't do the work, we'll find someone who can. I understand you have a difficult situation..."

"Sir, I promise I'll get everything done. I swear it."

"I'm giving you one last chance. Just get these assignments in today."

"Yes sir, thank you, sir," Shonali said, voice trembling.

With a loud click, her boss hung up, and Shonali was left alone on the dark staircase, the rush of rain resounding against the concrete. A deluge, a flood. Sliding down to sit on the stairs, Shonali cradled her head and one hand as she attempted to call her driver.

Three times, the phone rang, a bhajan echoing against the walls before a recorded voice began to say in Marathi, "I'm sorry, the person you are trying to reach..."

She wanted to slam her phone against the wall. To cry into her hands. It was too much. Yet whenever she closed her eyes, she saw her uncle's body lying there before her, blood mixed with rain.

She couldn't stay here. Not now, not with her uncle's blood still wet on the pavement.

Frustrated, she tried again but only received the same tepid message. Shonali would have to try again later. Or arrange for a new driver. Given the current downpour, the roads would be waterlogged. She logged into Uber and shifted through the prices and current drivers. She would go to another hotel, even if it were far away. To rest, to feel safe. Even if the price were double, she'd manage it, somehow.

Arranging a car, the app requested her credit card details. Rummaging in her bag for her wallet, she yanked it out, seeing only a few crumpled rupee notes and her credit and debit card.

She tried her credit card first. But it was declined. Frowning, she attempted the debit card.

Again, nothing.

Shonali cursed. Glancing at the back of the card, she called the helpdesk number and waited. Hold after hold, she listened to the sound of rain and tried to calm her breathing.

"Yes, we had a report of fraud on this card. So, it's currently disabled. You'll need to come to the branch to verify your identity and get your account unblocked."

"Ma'am, that's impossible. I'm currently in Mumbai and need the money on my card to get home."

"I'm sorry, but there's not much I can do."

Shivering, Shonali put her phone away and rubbed her wet eyes.

She was stuck.

Chapter 18
The Criteria

S honali had a day to spend in society. If she could at least get enough for train fare and auto back to Pune from her tenants and reduce their rent owed by that much, that would be a success.

But she couldn't bear to look at them again. Gita's zealous fawning and mothering now felt more than insincere. It was borderline claustrophobic. Every time she entered that damned flat, Shonali could almost feel a leathery grip on her throat, thumbs tight at the back of her neck.

So, instead, Shonali resolved to see Pooja Auntie. She made her way to the second building, careful of the deeper puddles, to the older woman's flat.

Pooja Desai was a member of the society committee and one of the longest-residing members there. Then, it only made sense that Pooja must know more than she admitted when Shonali first arrived. Shonali figured she could relay anything else to the investigator, Rudhrani, later. After all, this really wasn't just about her tenants anymore. A woman was missing, and a man was dead. Not to mention Mr. Kabraji's heart attack.

Approaching Pooja's door, Shonali could hear the melodious recording of Hemant Kumar flooding the flat and adjacent stairs. Yet, somehow, the older woman was able to hear her knock. Donning an apron and a bright yellow kurti, Pooja ushered Shonali inside with a large smile.

"Please, baito[1], baito," she motioned to a couch in front of a television, the news on mute. Shonali could see a report of rain damage and waterlogged streets. A man was wading fruitlessly through a gully, water up to his knees, umbrella blown back.

Similar to Kabrajis' flat, Pooja Desai's living room was dusty. A dead, gargantuan cockroach was sprawled on his back near the table, its hind legs still twitching, ants already lining up to yank flecks off its carcass. Shonali paled, staring at it, its soft underbelly concealing its hard brown shell.

"We just had the place fumigated a few days ago. In this climate, roaches come out. And the house lizards can only eat so many," Pooja sighed. "But I'm afraid the same poison killed the lizards, too."

"I remember. One summer, we had a terrible infestation," Shonali said weakly, taking a cup of chai. The woman put out a plate of soan papri and biscuits. "The tea is quite lovely."

"Thank you. I'm just finishing the daal. Would you like to stay? My husband went out again, it seems," muttered Pooja Auntie as she straightened her apron.

"No, thank you." Shonali urged her stomach not to growl. "I can't tell you fumigated at all. The smell is gone."

"Well, the solution is weaker than it used to be. And it was a few days ago. You'd be surprised what they found! There was a small cockroach nest near the sink, far back in the kitchen. We've had a house lizard, and we found him near there. I'm guessing he was picking off the little roaches one at a time, keeping them for feeding."

---

1. Baito - Hindi for the casual request to sit.

Shonali shivered at the thought, and Pooja seemed just as displeased.

"Of course, the man said that our house was one of the cleanest he had come across. Barely anything after that little nest. Those buggers just found one spot that we couldn't quite touch and multiplied. They only need a little space, and once they find it, they're in for life."

Shonali nodded, sipping at the hot tea.

"They come from the drain pipes, I believe. And the open windows."

"They come however you let them in. They find the darkest, dampest place in your home and build their own slimy place around it..."

Shivering, Shonali placed her cup and saucer on her lap. It was true—pest invasions began in such a way. Her mind wandered to the past, to that grueling summer, and her parents' unhappiness, that familial intolerance spinning out of control. Her father had accused her uncle of leaching off him.

Yet, that appeared now to be a loose projection. A kindling flame of greed, frustration, or even brotherly rivalry. If this flat wasn't even her father's and, therefore, wasn't hers, what right did she have? Who was infringing on whom?

There was something else, a secret, that was festering, infesting her future, and attracting maliciousness.

Shonali took a deep breath. She needed to focus on keeping herself and Pooja's Auntie on task. "Auntie, could I ask you what you honestly think of my tenants?"

The woman raised an eyebrow, but her back straightened. Her open expression drew back as she crossed her legs and shifted away from Shonali.

"I suppose they are good tenants. They follow all the rules."

"Yes, but what is your personal impression?" Shonali pressed cautiously.

Pooja shrugged. "They are good people." She placed her tea down, a faint pink lipstick outline on the rim. "They've really done a lot in the society itself. I've heard they are even getting us help."

"Getting help?"

"Well, all the maids quit. That's why it's so dusty," Pooja said, pursing her lips. "And the gardener. And most of the security. Don't quite know why. We had a bit of delay with payments, but these people are so finicky, you know."

Shonali bit her cheek. "Well, they do need to eat."

"Like the government doesn't give them anything," Pooja retorted. "In any case, Mrs. Bharadwaj told me they have a relative in an agency that assigns these tasks. So, they were able to bring their own people in at half the rate."

Shonali nodded dumbly.

"But isn't it odd that everyone left? Was it around the same time?"

"Yes, but it's not odd. These people stick together." Pooja shook her head. "People aren't like they used to be. Lazy. Rude. Money-hungry. Money is such a criteria these days, too."

Shonali's blood chilled, and she nearly dropped the chai and saucer. A few droplets of hot tea splattered on the back of her hand. Gita Bharadwaj had said the same exact thing.

"Pooja Auntie, since you are the committee, you should know that the Bharadwajs are in default on their rent."

"Oh, I'm sure they'll pay. They're good people," the woman rushed to say, her knuckles tight around her demitasse. "They're quite good tenants; they understand value. Families are always better. What if you had a bachelor? Or a young single woman? An extremist? Or a foreigner? Then we'd all have trouble. With your tenants, I wouldn't worry too much. They're quite well connected."

Shonali bit her lip. Apparently so. Hotels, staffing agencies—what else did they have their hands in? And while Worli was an affluent area, why squat in her little flat? There were certainly better options.

"They do seem quite well adjusted," Shonali admitted, if only to placate the woman. At her acquiescence, Pooja relaxed back into her chair, taking another sip of tea.

"Yes, and wealthy. That boy of theirs will be able to get quite a lot."

"You think so?"

"Well, they've already bought up half the remaining flats in the society. That's why this building is so quiet now."

Shonali furrowed her eyebrows.

"They've bought flats?"

"Yes. Raj's family owns a real estate firm. They have offices from Mumbai to Delhi. Buying all these flats must have cost them, too. And if they decide to fix them up, they will be spending even more. I might even sell while the market is good. Your tenants have also made a small donation to the society. How else would we be able to make repairs? So, you see. They'll likely get the rent straightened out soon enough."

Shonali frowned, the tea acidic in her gut. Suddenly, her hunger had vanished. Where did the maintenance and repair funds go that she paid every quarter, then, if not to repairs and paying staff? Why aren't they staying in or renting flats they've bought? She wanted to ask but bit her tongue. There was a vague possibility, one that seemed more and more real and yet just as impossible: They wanted leverage over her.

But for what?

"That's why I say not to worry, beta," Pooja seemed to relax. "Anyhow, we shouldn't gossip, should we? Let's talk about your family a bit. How are you doing?"

"Fine, fine. Father is fine," Shonali lied. No one was fine, not really, not now.

"Even after the stroke?"

"Yes," Shonali said quietly, wanting to curse. She needed to check up on her father, too.

"And your brother?"

"He's good, working hard," she replied. Yes, he was doing well for himself. Forget the money; he seemed completely unfettered by her burdens here. Free to live his life on his own terms. While Shonali was here, squeezing whatever information she could from people she now realized were far less genuine than she had initially believed.

"I'm sure." Pooja smiled widely. "And you? Any thoughts of getting married? You're about that age..."

"Not yet," Shonali smiled back, a tight, polite nod. "Soon, I'm sure. Thank you for the tea."

"You won't stay for lunch? You look famished. So thin."

Shonali straightened her dupatta and purse before standing up. "No, I really must be going. But, did you have a dog here?" Shonali asked, looking around. "I thought someone was missing. What was his name—Brinjal?"

At the mention of the little mutt, Pooja's face grew long. "I'm afraid he died about a month ago. He got sick all of a sudden." The woman's eyes were wet.

"Pooja Auntie, I'm so sorry," Shonali murmured.

"Of course, of course. It's fine. You didn't know," Pooja said, standing up. "Come again before you leave. We can chat more."

"I will," Shonali lied. She doubted she would be back. "And, before I go, I have one more quick question. Did you know why my uncle had been hanging around here lately?"

Pooja's face paled.

"Your uncle? I'm not sure what you mean. I haven't seen him in years," Pooja offered a brittle laugh as she opened the door.

When Shonali had asked her about the Bharadwaj family, anxiety had been written all over Pooja's face. But this was worse.

"Ah, well then, it must be my mistake," said Shonali as she left.

Despite what she had gleaned from Pooja, Shonali felt herself returning to her last conversation with Gita Bharadwaj. *Did you know him?* The woman had asked, knowingly, almost tauntingly.

How much did they know about her and her family? And how much power did they have over the remaining society members?

The watchman and Arjun had suggested that her uncle had visited several times before. Given the Bharadwaj family's recent *investments* in society, it made sense that they must have confronted her uncle at some point. Especially given their strict preferences for neighbors and personal associations.

Those people, they had kept saying. Pooja had said it, too.

And Shonali knew, at heart, what that meant. The dividing line was nearly invisible, festering beneath the surface of polite society, but never addressed, not talked about. And whatever they thought about Shonali, they were eager to condemn everyone around her.

Shonali returned to the Khan's flat, careful to be silent as she entered so as not to alert her tenants above. Sitting on the floor, she yanked out her phone and began scrolling through Facebook.

Finding her uncle's account was easy enough—she used the number he had given her before. Ignoring her growling stomach, she scanned the profile. His friend's list came up empty of any Bharadwaj.

But his timeline was full of warm wishes and "get well soon" comments.

The reason he had been adamant about meeting her father became immediately clear.

Her uncle had been dying of cancer.

Seeing a photograph of him at the hospital, with a caption about chemotherapy, guilt began to seep in.

True, they had been estranged. She remembered the tenor of her father's yelling, the clash of broken glasses and her mother muttering about her uncle's insobriety under her breath. Shouldn't they have been there for her uncle despite his faults? But she didn't have an answer now, and she likely never would.

Frowning, she dialed Rudhrani's number.

"Are you still in Mumbai?"

"Unfortunately not. I had to take a last-minute trip to Pune," Rudhrani sighed. "It's a long story but I'll be finishing up some inquiries from there. Did you find anything else?"

"No, not quite. But if I give you my address, could you check on my father? My neighbor will let you in."

"Alright. Anything else?"

"While you are there, could you look through the records in the cabinet in the hall? They are in a black messenger bag in a red folder labeled "Golden Deer." It's quite large. It has all the documentation about this house. But there might be another one with other documents. Ones I haven't seen."

"Okay. Got it. Black bag, red folder," the investigator repeated back.

"And my uncle," Shonali felt her voice stick in her throat. "My uncle has—had—been hanging around the gate of the society, apparently. I don't know how long. But he was found dead today."

There was a slow inhale on the other line. Then, a cough.

"Your uncle is dead?"

"My brother said he was a partial owner of the house. I just found out last night. And this morning, the police were here. They found his body at the gate. And I think...I think my tenants knew that he was my uncle."

"The Bharadwajs?"

"Yes."

"Did the police question you?"

"Not yet."

"Good. Just... keep me updated. And text me your address here in Pune. I'll swing by and check on everything. Please grant me permission to enter and investigate your home, too. Send me a video on WhatsApp. For the watchman and anyone else," the investigator requested.

"Of course. Thanks."

"And, are *you* doing okay?"

The concern in her voice nearly broke Shonali, the sobs catching in her chest.

"Once this is all over, I'll feel better," she admitted, rubbing tears from her eyes. "Is there anyone I can talk to here, do you think? About potential records?"

"Well, whoever is managing your society should have copies of the shared certificates, among other things. Maybe your broker, if you've used one," Rudhrani replied.

Shonali hung up and sent her a brief video requesting that the watchman give Rudhrani Sen access. She leaned back to lean against the sofa, her stomach growling. Once the rain let up, she would walk to the cafe from yesterday. For now, she would work. And tonight, she would sleep again in the Khan residence. If Rudhrani was in Mumbai, she could catch a ride home with her back to Pune once this was resolved. Sighing, she plugged her phone into the charger and began editing again, her mind racing.

Despite the progress she had made, despite the new information she had collected, deep in her belly, Shonali knew that her uncle's death would not be the end of this.

Chapter 19
The Father

Rudhrani firmly believed that there was such a thing as luck—and that she did not have it. After speaking with Shonali, she felt the momentum building for the case. She had made copies of Gauri Bhave's documents and sent digital pictures of them to a friend in Pune, as well as to the local Mumbai officer contact.

The bottle of pills, too, she had compared with a fresh bottle at three different pharmacies. While she was unable to get a drug test at the moment, the freshly packaged pills were noticably different in color and size to those Gauri had given her.

She seemed to be making progress.

But then her brother called. Her mother had taken a serious fall the night before. And she knew then that while there was much she wanted to do in Mumbai, that she was needed at home. And so, after dropping off the suspect pill bottle at the police station, Rudhrani drove back to Pune to see her mother. She suffered a fracture in her arm and would need as much rest as possible.

Advice, Rudhrani knew, her mother would immediately reject. Walking in the door, she could hear the microwave running and her mother asking if she was okay with leftover okra.

Shonali's call, just as she had booked a cab to return to Pune, had thrown her off completely. And the entire ride, all she could think about was Sujoy Chatterjee. How paranoid he really had been, if at all? His death could hardly be labeled as a coincidence.

The only positive development was that Shonali could investigate on the ground in Mumbai and that Rudhrani may get access to information from Shonali's flat under the guise of visiting her father.

Immediately after eating and ensuring her mother was okay, Rudhrani drove to Shonali's home.

Entering Shonali's flat was hardly difficult. It was a small, two-bedroom apartment on the western side of the city. When she knocked on the neighbor's door, she had her WhatsApp ready to show them. Hopefully, this would be a quick in-and-out situation, and she could get back to Mumbai.

But that wasn't the case.

The elderly woman cracked open the door, staring at the stranger in front of her.

"I'm Rudhrani—I think Shonali must have messaged you. I'm here to check on her father."

At this, the woman smiled sweetly and opened the door fully. Rudhrani could see her fiddling with a small rack of keys on the wall, feeling the edges of each individual key before finally finding the right one.

"Shonali's such a sweet girl. She cares so much about her father. We've been checking on him thrice a day. Can you believe that maid just abandoned him? Will you be checking on him every day going forward?"

"No, just today," Rudhrani said as they approached the door. "Didn't the maid have an emergency?"

"You know they all say that," the woman sighed. "They just want more time off. But it's better to have a nurse checking in, isn't it?" The woman looked at her as they reached the door. "After all, the doctor can't come every day."

"The doctor?"

"Yes, a man came the other day, saying he was a doctor, and Shonali asked him to visit. It wasn't the first time a doctor had been to the house. I didn't just let him in, of course. But he spoke so well as if he knew her and her brother. I figured it was alright to let him in."

"Around what time did he come?"

"Around eleven, just before lunch," the woman returned to the door, twisting the key in the heavy lock. "Should I not have let him in?" A look of mortification suddenly passed by her features.

"He might have been the doctor," Rudhrani said calmly. "I'd have to ask Shonali. Did you go in with him?"

"No, no. I was cooking and couldn't be away for too long. I did take the keys with me, and I saw him get in the elevator and leave."

Rudhrani frowned. Who knows if there was an extra key in the house that he might have taken? Shonali certainly hadn't mentioned anyone, and if a doctor had come to check on her father, there would be little reason to ask Rudhrani to come beyond the papers.

The investigator thanked the woman, reassuring her that everything was likely fine, and then entered the flat. There was a thin layer of dust that had accumulated over the past few days. Cautiously, she peeked into every room. But beyond Shonali's father seemingly sleeping, the slow rise and fall of his chest barely noticeable underneath a thin blue sheet, there was no one else in the home.

Then she headed for the teak cabinet Shonali had mentioned. Ruffling through a stack of papers and files, she noticed a bulky black briefcase with a red folder labeled "Golden Deer" sticking precariously out of its mouth. Inside was a thin book of photos of the flat, emptied of furniture, no doubt to compare for when tenants moved out and to assess potential damage. But the rest of the documents are of little interest. Utility bills, paid society dues, former tenant agreements. Nothing that could prove undeniable ownership.

Frowning, she began to ruffle through the other papers. There were copies of everything and anything that could be used for documentation—birth certificates, ID cards, PAN cards, school leaving certificates, passbooks, resumes, work letters, pay stubs, and so on.

But there was one thing missing. Proof of ownership of *this* flat. Nowhere was there an original copy of an Index-II, probably one of the most accepted and essential documents for proving residency.

Leaning back onto her knees, the tile floor groaning under her weight, Rudhrani surveyed the room, looking for any nook or cranny that might contain additional documents. Shonali said there might be some tucked away in the house.

Then she heard a quiet, stressed hum, almost like a whine. She shot up and went to the bedroom. Shonali's father stared at her from his lying position, eyes wide.

"I'm your daughter's friend," Rudhrani said calmly, cautiously. "She wanted me to come check on you."

He hummed again, but the desperation didn't leave his gaze. The anguish at being unable to move, to communicate something so obviously worrisome.

"The neighbor said someone entered the house the other day. Blink twice if that's true," said the investigator. And he did. "For now on, blink twice if the answer is yes. Three times if the answer is no. Did you know the man?" There were three blinks. "Was he a doctor?" Another three blinks. "Did he hear about the Mumbai flat?" To her disappointment, it was another three blinks. She would need to deal with that later—she couldn't be guessing topics over and over, hoping to pinpoint them.

"Are there original papers about the Mumbai flat?" Two blinks. "Are they in this room?" Another yes. Rudhrani glanced around the room. There was a vast array of modular storage spaces under the bed, jutting from the wall over pink-painted metal cabinets. She asked about each place until, eventually, she hit a yes. The cabinet.

Opening the cabinet door, it was filled with clothes. Piles of shirts and pants, hangers sagging with ties. And a small safe requiring a key. A key that was still in the lock.

She opened it carefully. There were several boxes of jewelry stacked on top of each other. Small gold coins still in packets, barely 0.2 grams apiece. And a manila envelope. She took it out in front of Mr. Chatterjee and gingerly opened it.

Inside were a couple of ratty documents outside of the original passport copies and IDs. A share certificate of the Mumbai flat, last updated over a decade ago, granting ownership to two sons. An unprobated will was signed by Shonali's father, uncle, and a lawyer. An aged photograph of three young men, two of whom she immediately recognized. Shonali's father and his brother Sujoy. The third man bore a resemblance to both, and she could only imagine him to be the third brother, the one Shonali barely knew.

But there was nothing definite she could use.

"And the documents for this flat?"

The man managed a garbled word. *Taken.*

Rudhrani placed the documents on the bed and walked back to him. He could talk then, but not much. Not well enough to be understood clearly. Despite his feebleness, he was alert. Completely conscious and aware of his predicament. And no doubt why the man had come the day before.

"H...hand," he said.

Looking down at his hands, both lying at his sides, Rudhrani could immediately tell what he was referring to. On the pad of his right thumb was a thin layer of black residue. Ink.

The man had taken a fingerprint.

"Did the man have you sign something with your fingerprint?"

He gurgled, blinking twice.

"Where are the papers regarding this flat?"

Another yes. She got up and took the folder of originals. Thumbing through them, she realized the PAN card and passport were missing. And she had seen them in the copies.

"Did he say anything?"

Three blinks. No.

"Did he clean everything up before he left?"

A yes.

Rudhrani's mind began to whirl. Her temples tingled. It was the edge of clarity. Even without clear links between events and characters, the investigator was on the precipice of knowing.

The only thing she needed now was a little more time.

Ruffling in her purse, she yanked out a journal and a pen. Then, she began scanning her contact list. Soon, she would need to call the junior police officer in Mumbai once again. But first, Rudhrani needed a confirmation. And for that, there was an old friend she needed to follow up with— a former batchmate she had sent Gauri's documents to.

And, of course, her brother, who could help her with some additional paperwork.

Chapter 20
The Paperwork

S honali reclined on the couch weakly as she finished the salted peanut packet beside her. Mrs. Bharadwaj had messaged her during the day, saying it was better to stop by the next day as her husband wouldn't be home until morning.

And while she wasn't paying for a hotel, Shonali felt a twist in her gut at leaving her father for so long. The only update she had about his well-being was a brief text from Rudhrani, simply stating that he seemed 'fine.' On the flip side, the investigator also said she was working on a lead—so not all was lost.

But all the same, Shonali found herself in an intense brain fog. Lack of sleep, an empty stomach, and a full day's work had drained her entirely. While her migraines were at bay, she found herself unwilling to move until she finally convinced herself to shower.

Of course, to her frustration, the shower head had long been clogged with dried salt and minerals from hard water. Only three small streams sputtered from the shower. Scratching her eyes, Shonali brought the bucket closer to the faucet and let it fill to the brim before quickly washing it.

The cold water energized her—but only so much that she could redress and drag herself back to the sofa. She couldn't bring herself to try sleeping in the Khans' bedroom. It felt far too personal, too much of a trespass.

Curling on the couch, she recited the Hanuman Chalisa as she fell into sleep. Tomorrow would be different. It had to be.

Just as she felt her muscles relax and sleep tapered over her eyes and drew her closer, a resounding bang clashed and echoed against the walls.

She squinted her eyes open. Two glowing, red eyes watched her from close to the ceiling. Chest constricting, gooseflesh cold and taut, Shonali could barely breathe.

Then she saw it. And sighed in relief.

The lights were linked to a small inverter on a custom shelf. The power must have gone.

She heard, then, the pitter-patter of feet outside in the stairwell.

Sitting up, Shonali peeked outside the little hole in the door.

Nothing. Not a soul.

The fluorescent light reflected hard against the concrete, the lack of natural lighting only intensifying its glare. Shonali frowned and moved away, her eyes readjusting to the dark flat.

Again, a thump above her. Then, one below.

She wanted to scream.

Shonali dragged herself back to the couch and placed a pillow over her head, hoping to drown out the sounds. In her state, the whole world seemed topsy-turvy. With the rain, the shadows swayed, the branches adding to the cacophony of noises. She laid on her back and tried again to sleep to block out the noise.

Shonali got up again and flicked on a light, which cracked and expired immediately, leaving her in the dark.

Again, the thump of footsteps outside the door. Heavier this time. Shonali lay still, anxiety creeping into her chest.

There was a pause. Then, a second set of steps. It was faint, but she could hear the sound of anklets clinking. And a low murmur.

Slowly, Shonali got up again and approached the door. The thin light filtering under the frame abruptly vanished, leaving her in darkness. The last phase must have gone now, too. Shonali looked through the peephole.

In the darkness, it all appeared empty.

Shonali wanted to scream in frustration. Instead, she wiped her strained, sleepless eyes.

She would ignore everything. And, somehow, she did. Wrapping herself in a blanket on the couch, Shonali watched the door until her body gave out.

Eventually, dawn arrived, and it did so with a clash of cries and shouts from outside the building. Shonali turned over, forgetting she was on the couch; she nearly lost her balance and dropped to the ground. She couldn't remember when she had finally drifted off into an exhausted sleep, but she certainly hadn't slept long enough.

She pulled herself to the window. Rain and thick branches veiled her sight. Only a small figure could be seen, and only because the stark blackness stuck out against the fuzzy gray light. Frowning, Shonali watched the outline, waiting for it to move. But it did nothing. And nothing intercepted it.

The entire garden and car park were silent. The yelling that had awoken her had dissipated as if in a dream.

Shonali slipped on her mostly dry sandals and picked up her umbrella. Tiptoeing out of the flat, she quietly ventured down the steps, each turn of the staircase knotting her stomach, making her anxiety spiral.

From the ground, she could see that the outline was a person on the ground, sprawled out, water sloshing around him. Almost dropping the umbrella, Shonali felt herself quickening her pace, only to slow down again from a sudden bout of dizziness.

Gingerly sitting beside the body, Shonali could see him clearly. It was the watchman. Deftly, she took his pulse. It was weak but still there. He had a gnarled gash on his forehead, wet blood mixed with rain sliding down his face.

Yanking her phone out, she called the emergency number and waited. The rain chilled her clothes to the bone as she sat with him, keeping the umbrella over his face.

Her eyes searched the windows. Was there no one else up? Someone had to be— there had been so much noise just a few minutes ago.

But not a single soul was visible. The rain hindered her vision, but she couldn't discover a single out-of-place silhouette in the car park. Each window appeared black and empty. For the first time, she fully absorbed the significance of the lack of houseplants and curtains on the window sills, of the absolute isolation that enveloped her. She tried to count the members of the crowd from when her uncle had been found. There had been a measly four or five people, including Arjun and Mohan, the watchman, the latter now unconscious before her.

Shonali tried to speak to him, but he was nearly lifeless, only a weak pulse providing any hope of recovery. Taking her dupatta from her shoulders, she folded it hastily to put under his head, to at least shield it from the water and the cold.

Shonali wasn't certain how long she waited there for the ambulance to arrive. But like the night with Kabraji, like with her uncle, strewn at the gate, eventually, a stretcher arrived.

"Is he going to be okay?"

"You should have pulled him in somewhere warm," the paramedic reprimanded her as he stuffed the stretcher into the ambulance.

"I couldn't, all by myself."

The paramedic weighed her response, his eyes wandering over her thin figure. He agreed with his silence. Shonali was half the man's weight, at least. Her thin arms struggled with the full pressure cooker half the time, let alone carrying a grown man to the stairwells several meters away.

"Can I come?"

"Are you family?"

Shonali shook her head but looked at him pleadingly.

"Then no."

The man was ready to shut the door to the ambulance. Digging through her pockets, she quickly found a one-hundred rupee note and shoved it toward his chest. A poor bribe, but it was something. The man only rolled his eyes, took the note, and promptly slammed the door. With the back door shut, the ambulance bolted off down the gate and around the corner.

Picking up her soiled pink dupatta from the wet gravel, she brushed off the leaves and twigs and water from it. The pale cream color was now gray and black from soil and grease. Sighing, Shonali returned to the stairs and sat, legs shaking.

She fidgeted for a few minutes before finally pulling out her phone again and calling her brother.

"What is it, Shonali? Are you in Pune?"

"No." Her voice was trembling, lips cold. "Ajit, the watchman died. Or was hit? I don't know."

"What?"

"The watchman and our uncle," mumbled Shonali. Her heartbeat pulsed in her ears as the deaths merged together just as the blood streaked with the rain.

"Slow down, speak clearly. What happened?"

"The other day, our uncle died near the gate. And now the watchman, I found him this morning, bleeding out in front of the society. He had been assaulted." Tears were rolling down her cheeks now.

"Okay, okay, hold on," her brother said, shuffling sounds mixing with his curses. "What time is it there?"

"I don't know. The sun was rising when I woke up."

"Shonali, Shonali, don't get hysterical," he sighed.

"I'm not hysterical! A man was dying in front of me. Our uncle died! And Mrs. Khan is missing," Shonali wept. "Something's wrong here. Someone is doing this. The tenants are involved. I know it."

There was a huff at the other end of the line. "Why would they do this? Are you hearing yourself?"

"I don't know. Not yet, but—"

"No buts. It was probably bad luck. The man probably had a heart attack and fell. Now relax and go sleep it off. You're stressed. You're losing it again. Making up stories and excuses, just like before exams."

"Ajit, I'm serious. Don't you think it's odd—"

"A few coincidences and bad luck don't mean a thing. You're being ridiculous," her brother chastised her. She could hear the frustration laced in his voice. "Besides, I bet you are seeing cockroaches and some other stupid bugs again, aren't you? Are those nightmares back?"

Shonali didn't say a single word, feeling the breath knocked out of her. Her sobbing stopped, but only because her body didn't have the energy to express her terror, her fatigue. She sat still, cold and numb, leaning against the wall.

"That's what I thought. Look, go home. I'll wire some money tomorrow."

"My account is frozen," she replied weakly.

"What?"

"The bank said suspicious activity," Shonali hiccupped. "I have to go to the branch."

"How much do you have on you?"

"Not a lot. Just enough for food."

"Fuck's sake, Shonali," her brother said. He muttered a few more curses under his breath. "You're useless, you know that? Without me, everything falls apart."

It wasn't the first time he cursed at her, but the vulgarity shook her, if only because his rage and cruelty were unfounded. So callous and unwarranted.

"You should carry more with you, going to Mumbai..."

"I didn't have so much more! We're already maxing out credit to eat and pay maintenance fees."

"Default then!"

"I can't do that," Shonali sighed. And she didn't have the credit for a loan.

"No one will evict you. We own the flat in Pune, fees be damned," her brother said, as if off-hand. As if it was so easy.

"You don't know that. You don't know what it's like over here. I'm alone with our father, Ajit. You don't know what it takes to take care of him."

"Fire the maid then."

"I'm not talking about just money!" Shonali wanted to rip her hair out. "And even then, I let her go months ago. I only rehired her for this trip," Shonali moaned. "God, Ajit, the answer isn't getting rid of people. I'm already so alone. I need some support." Her voice faded. She needed something. Just until all this was over. Until her paycheck came in, and the rent money was returned. Until she got rid of the stupid flat.

"And I'll send it," Ajit spat out. "Just get a hold of yourself and get back to Pune. Go to the branch as soon as you can, and fix the problem. Okay?"

Shonali nodded quietly before hanging up the phone. Her hands were chilled from the rain. Rubbing them against her eyes, she clicked her tongue. He was right about one thing. Shonali needed to get the money straightened out. But how long would that last?

Whether he believed her or not, something strange was also going on in her flat. There was something wrong with the flat itself. And she was going to figure it out.

Fuck Ajit and his money.

Shonali needed to know for herself what happened to Mrs. Khan. To the other residents and tenants. And why Pooja was so eager to praise the Bharadwajs?

And it all linked back to these strangers her brother had so carelessly let into their home.

Wiping her face, Shonali called Kaushik, who ignored her. She followed up with the broker her brother and father had used to find their current tenants, Krishna Gaikwad. He answered after two calls but deferred her to his colleague, Amar Mir, who had been the previous broker for the area.

Amar had, before their deal with the Bharadwajs, helped her father to manage the property. Once Shonali explained her situation, in brief, he picked her up from the society gate and took her to the real estate office.

Polite and resourceful, Amar asked her to sit in the office as he called on Kaushik again. She listened while daintily sipping on bottled water, trying to make it last.

"I thought you had left Mumbai," Shonali said quietly as if trying to shrink herself further.

"No, not at all. It's my home. But yours is a difficult situation," Amar responded, mildly surprised by her comment. "I worked with your father for years on maintaining the flat. Normally under-the-table deals—he never wanted to pay for stamp duty. But we'll get this sorted."

"Is there anything we can do? About the tenants?"

"Well, you're not charging enough to get gangsters to rough them up. Getting them involved will eat up all of your rent money," he said thoughtfully. Shonali had the feeling he wasn't joking. "And legally, you can't cut water or electricity. So, we just have to make them pay or wait for them to move out."

"So, they can squat, technically."

Amar shifted uncomfortably. "Legally, they can't. But if you try to take this to court, it can take years to actually get them removed. So, unless they decide to leave, it's a bit of an impasse."

"Do you have any papers here that could help?"

"Like?"

"I'm not sure," Shonali confessed. "Records? The share certificates?"

"I just have copies of old agreements." The broker sighed, leaning back in his chair. "Ideally, you'll want the will of your grandfather, ideally a probated one, who I believe left the flat to your father. Kaushik should be bringing whatever records he has."

"I think my uncle had some ownership before. But we bought back his shares," Shonali said.

"If that's true, you'd need registration and stamp duty papers to prove that. And an updated share certificate," said Amar as he scribbled notes in an open-lined notebook.

Shonali sipped on her water. That was quite a lot of paperwork she would need. They waited, wallowing in small talk, for Kaushik to eventually arrive.

And the man did, arriving in the same foul mood as before. He glared at Shonali before Amar put a two-hundred rupee note in his palm, which immediately transformed his entire attitude. Kaushik folded the note carefully as Amar reviewed the papers and made copies. Shonali leaned forward in her seat, anxiously watching his expressions.

His frown did not give her a good impression of the state of affairs.

"There is a will that leaves it to both brothers, but it's not probated," he sighed.

"Not a third brother, too?" Shonali asked tentatively. She remembered her father's elder brother.

Amar glanced up at her, exasperated. "No, no one else is listed here. Do you have a reason he'd have a say in this?"

"No, he disappeared a long time ago. I don't even know if he's alive."

Perhaps he disappeared before the inheritance was passed on, Shonali reasoned. That was the only explanation she could think of. Distancing her uncle, Sujoy, Shonali could understand. Even when she met him outside the society, she scented the memory of whiskey—a destructive alcoholic. And the elder brother could have been the same, or worse. How would she know? She had never met him.

The agent shrugged. "Nothing like that. There are just two names here on the will. There is a shared certificate with your father's name but no registration. No stamp duty. Nothing that legally ties the property to your father alone. Unless you have this for your flat, it's going to be incredibly hard to ever sell your property. Once your tenants move out, of course."

Chapter 21
The Scheme

B ack at the Khan's flat and dripping wet from the rain, Shonali sat on the floor and counted her remaining funds. She only had around 500 rupees in cash. Checking her phone, she also had barely 200 rupees in her digital wallet. There was just enough for a small meal, a train ride, and an Uber to get to and from the station.

Leaving her dupatta in the bathroom to dry, Shonali went to the cafe again, this time to warm up and eat. The cashier looked at her up and down. It was the same worker who had been there the day before. Shonali could tell the woman recognized her, and there was no doubt she also realized that Shonali was wearing the same sopping wet clothes from before, too.

Choosing the cheapest tea and sandwich, Shonali sat in the far corner, away from the windows. She crossed her arms over her chest, shivering, cursing herself for forgetting that the cafe had air conditioning. Once all of this was over, Shonali wouldn't be surprised if she came down with a severe cold.

A few minutes later, when the girl came with her sandwich, there were two tightly nestled together on the plate. She hadn't ordered the more expensive grilled option, but the bread had been pressed, and steam wafted from the cheesy edges.

"Don't worry about it. It's covered," the woman said sheepishly before returning behind the counter.

The kind gesture was enough to warm Shonali's hopes. Checking her phone, she found that Rudhrani had not only pinged her but called a few times.

"Are you sitting down?"

Shonali was grateful she hadn't started eating; otherwise, she might have choked.

"Is my father okay?"

"Oh, yes, he's fine," Rudhrani said. "But I've got a huge info dump for you. I don't have *all* the details. But I've been at it all night. "She muffled a heavy cough.

"Are *you* okay?"

"Fine, fine. Don't stress about that. We need to talk about your flat in Pune."

"There's nothing wrong with the Pune flat. We own it," Shonali said before taking a bite of the sandwich.

"Yeah, not for long."

Shonali felt the mayonnaise from the sandwich curdle in her mouth.

"Apparently, some man came to your flat the day before I did and got your father's thumbprint, and I have a feeling it was on a sales deed. The Index-IIs and other documentation regarding the flat are missing, too.

"I have a friend working in real estate, and he spent all day yesterday helping me track down as much of that information as possible. Of course, it helped that your society committee had some copies on file, too."

"What will I owe him?" Shonali was thankful for his help. But even with the kindness of strangers, it was hard to shake the impulse that nothing was truly free.

Rudhrani chuckled. "Nothing, it's pro bono. He had a crush on me in the eleventh standard, and I think he still does." Rudhrani said before clearing her throat. "Anyway, there are two things we found. One is that your flat is being sold to Padma Properties. It's the same company that's been buying out flats in your society. But this isn't the only thing. They also took an imprint for the Pune flat."

"Can they do that? Why would they do that?"

"Well, now that your uncle is dead and your father owns the flat, there's no competition. So, yes, if he agrees to transfer ownership—which he legally can't. But no one is going to check at this point. My guess is that this company is related to Dilip Kapoor and your tenants, and they might even have some connections in the land registration offices who can push it through. Bribery or otherwise."

"Okay, but why? Why go through all this trouble? Wouldn't it be easier to just buy the flats?"

"Easier but more expensive. Think about it this way: If they pay off someone for 50,000 rupees, force someone to sell their flat at a reduced price, or, in your case, cut you out of a deal entirely, they'd make a killing. After all, flats in Mumbai can easily go for 10,000,000[1] or more."

Shonali paused. So, in theory, it was all about money.

"Right. If that's true, can we stop them?"

Shonali wanted to be rid of the flat. But not like this. Not in a state where she loses everything. Where would her dad go? Where would she go? It wasn't like Ajit could bring them to America—even if he wanted to.

"Yes, well, I'm working on that. It's pretty underhanded. You need to be careful."

---

1. 10,000,000 - 1 crore rupees, around $120,200 USD as of 2023

Shonali gulped, the white bread dry and scratching her throat.

"If this is a land grab scheme, it's pretty well organized. They've probably done this more than once. I need more time to gather evidence and validate the legal loopholes. But you could have a case." Rudhrani's faint, optimistic tone was more of a question than a certainty.

"But a case would take years," whispered Shonali. She didn't have that kind of time. Or that kind of money.

"Yeah."

"Where would I live? What if they evict me?"

"It would cost a lot to evict you, even if you tried to squat. I mean, hiring a gang would probably cost twenty or thirty thousand alone," Rudhrani said offhand. Apparently, everyone but Shonali knew the price of hiring gundhas. "But if they plan to sell it, it's possible this type of eviction is worth the money. It's really hard to say."

"I don't...we don't have anywhere to go. We don't have any money, really," Shonali said, despondency creeping in. This forceful takeover, combined with the lack of proper documentation, would result in a poor case. How could she convince the government of the Mumbai flat's ownership when her parents hadn't even properly registered the property? Especially if she couldn't protect their own paperwork-verified flat in Pune?

Then there was Nazia Khan. Who still was missing.

"And what about Nazia? Or the other tenants? Is this a pattern? Is she okay?" The questions tumbled out of her like water from a broken dam.

"I'm still working on that. The police wouldn't get involved until I had proof she was missing. Your experience and what I've learned from some other tenants—that's enough to get the police to look for her.

"You also need to be safe. I don't think you should confront your tenants or anyone else in the society for the time being. Not only may they be responsible for Mrs. Khan, but there's been at least one murder—using poisoned pills. And probably another, if we count your uncle."

"And the watchman," said Shonali, rubbing her forehead. "I found him with a gash on his head outside. I can't imagine that's unrelated."

Rudhrani cursed over the phone.

"So what can I do now, Rudhrani? I'm out of money, my bank accounts are frozen, and I don't have anywhere to go. I've been living out of Asha's flat," Shonali said, each word a hammer nailing numbness into her chilled skin.

If there was a home to come back to. Shonali licked her dry lips and took a sip of tea as Rudhrani coughed.

"Shonali, let me find some leverage. Just don't interact with the Bharadwajs until I get something. Or Kapoor if you see him. If I need to wire you something, let me know."

"Are you sure?"

"Of course. You're my client, too, now," Rudhrani said.

She was so tired of crying, but Shonali wanted to weep there in the corner of the cafe, not just because of the helplessness she felt but also because of the support she'd received from strangers. The broker, Amar, Rudhrani—even the worker here had all been more supportive than her own flesh and blood.

But Shonali couldn't put the onus of fighting on everyone else. Not when she had come this far, not when her livelihood was at stake.

"This would be a big story for the papers, wouldn't it?"

"What are you thinking?" Rudhrani said, caution laced in her voice. "Journalism isn't exactly safe, either. Making things public could put them on the offensive."

"But... it would put pressure on them, right?" Shonali responded. "I could pitch it to the editor I work under and see if he takes it, even if someone else writes it."

Her boss wouldn't be keen on her writing. But this was a big story, a serious story. For a local paper barely staying afloat, this would sell.

Rudhrani seemed to be thinking if silence was any indication.

"That might warn them in advance. But it's a strategy all the same. Is the paper you work for any good?"

"They're all right, the crime coverage, anyway. I've met the team a few times. They aren't afraid to get their hands dirty. It just depends on the editor," said Shonali.

"Well, all right. But make sure to keep your name out of it, okay?" Rudhrani paused again. "This is serious. You shouldn't put yourself in danger."

When the private investigator hung up, Shonali sighed in quasi-relief. She wasn't alone in this. Yet, the entire situation was a terrible turn of events.

Embroiled in this scam, Shonali wanted to scream. She didn't even want the damn house. Her parents had bickered over its management countless times. It had been the bane of her mother's existence while she had been alive.

And now *everything* was on the line.

But at least she could do something, no matter how small.

Taking a deep breath, Shonali rang up her editor and waited. Life was coursing through her again. The conversation with Rudhrani had invigorated her senses, giving her, no matter how minuscule, a purpose and an approach.

"Shonali," her editor quipped impatiently. "I've got your files..."

"Look, sir, I have a big story."

"Shonali, what did I tell you?" he snapped.

"Please, sir, I don't have to write it. But it's a big scoop for your crime branch."

He consented with an impatient huff. And in haste, she explained, trying to summarize what she had just learned, that a group was conning people out of real estate, most likely from those unable to care for themselves. Squatting, then pressuring them out of their homes. That she had firsthand knowledge of the actors.

And when she had finished, she was met with silence. Then, a sigh.

"Shonali, I don't know what you are doing in Mumbai."

"Sir—"

"No, now you listen. I listened to your bogus story. Do you think a scam this big could really get past the main papers? The government? And, anyway, bringing in one of the shareholders into this is really troublesome."

"Shareholders?"

"One of the main investors, Kapoor, his brother, is a big fish. He's involved in the paper. Just became a majority stakeholder six months ago. And they've got close connections in politics around here. Don't tell me you didn't know?"

Shonali felt her mouth go dry.

"Look, I won't go around telling them you said any of this because, as far as I am concerned, you no longer work here."

"Sir—"

"Goodbye, Shonali. Talk to HR about your payments."

With a click, her boss was gone.

Shonali sat there, astounded. She had the scoop of the decade. And the damn family had their hands in the paper.

Who else did they own?

She wanted to beat her head against the wall. What little hope Shonali had left was dashed. It was as if she was locked away in an endless loop in this society, trapped in a circle her family had left her in. And somehow, she was expected to keep them going, as if with her own life. Now jobless, Shonali was truly dependent on her brother and this stupid, cursed flat for payment.

Shonali placed the hot demitasse against her jaw to ease the tension.

No.

She wasn't going to give up like this. She wasn't going to let them win—any of them.

Not her brother. Not the Bharadwajs. Not the Kapoors.

Shonali was going to expose this all.

Not because she wanted the damn flat, but because she wanted to live.

Chapter 22
The Struggle

The only thing to do, in Shonali's estimation, was to face the target head-on.

The risks, if the Bharadwajs were indeed behind any of the suspicious attacks in the society, were high. But she couldn't handle it anymore. Shonali knew she didn't have the stamina or mental acumen for games—not as things stood, with her starved and tired.

At least Shonali could get them to admit something. She could record them. And that had to count for something.

After returning to the flat, Shonali charged her phone and readied a recording app. She also installed another application for safety, ready to alert Rudhrani and Asha if she hadn't messaged them by eight p.m. She glanced at the wall clock every other moment, her palms sweating.

Grooming herself as best as she could, Shonali approached the flat in the early evening, hiding at the top of the stairs near the terrace, and waited until she noticed Arjun leave in the car park. Then, she finally tiptoed to Flat 501.

Mrs. Bharadwaj was entirely alone. She answered the door, her face pinched in a polite but stretched smile as she ushered Shonali in.

"How nice of you to visit. I'm afraid my husband isn't here. Wouldn't it be more convenient for you to return home until we can sort out this mess?" She played with her bangles, almost disinterested. "I'm afraid I'm out of tea. I can get you sherbet?"

"Nothing, thank you. I'll wait."

Shonali leaned back on the divan, watching the woman. In a fight, Shonali knew she would lose. Mrs. Bharadwaj was lean but well-fed and healthy.

"The gas smell is still here," said Shonali disapprovingly.

"Is it? I'm afraid I don't smell it at all," the woman retorted. "I've been cooking all day. Do you cook?"

"Of course. What makes you think I don't cook?"

"No need to get rude," Mrs. Bharadwaj bristled. "Goodness, this rain... we need it, but it's so heavy these days."

"It really is. I keep thinking that it must be hard for those thrown out of their homes."

Mrs. Bharadwaj's eyes sharpened into a piercing glare.

"Yes, it's unfortunate. But some people just enjoy living in filth."

"Tell me, what do you determine to be filth?"

"You're a good girl, aren't you? It should be obvious, but it appears your parents haven't taught you anything about one's duty."

"I only wanted to know *your* thoughts, Auntie. I'm sure we agree on many such topics," Shonali said, feigning curiosity. Mrs. Bharadwaj's wariness didn't falter, but the answer seemed to appease her somewhat.

A crack of thunder interrupted the tension, and the lights flickered. Shonali noticed thin rolling water streaks, like snakes, slithering down from the ceiling. It wouldn't surprise her if the deluge brought the ceiling down.

"This really is an old flat. I'm surprised you can squeeze twenty thousand out of us for this."

"We had repaired the terrace before the rains to ensure that it wouldn't leak. Replastered and added sandbags above," replied

Shonali. "And of course, the upkeep, brokerage, taxes, and utilities come to 18,000 rupees. So, it's more than fair."

The woman shrugged off her explanation as the lights went out. In the dark, Mrs. Bharadwaj looked less fair and more of a sickly, jaundiced shade, her eyes still glinting.

"My son should be home any minute."

"That's good. I need to speak with Arjun and your husband."

"Again, unless the banks have let up, there's nothing I can do."

"You're saying that you only have one family bank account? You don't have one in your name?"

"Of course, but it's for household goods. For the family," Gita Bharadwaj said, her voice growing louder. "You'll understand when you're married."

"I suppose."

"But it'll be hard for you if you can't understand others' positions," Mrs. Bharadwaj chastised. "A woman is a pillar for the husband and her children, you know. She should be able to manipulate them as well as take care of them. It's her duty."

Shonali shivered at her words.

"And, of course, you should be willing to learn under your mother-in-law. But I feel that you might want one of the less responsible women, I suppose. Without any kind of dignity." Gita Bharadwaj snorted, adjusting her mangalsutra.

"Respect and trust are really the most important things for me," said Shonali sternly. "A person or family without a sense of respect aren't really good people, are they?"

Mrs. Bharadwaj's carefully manicured eyebrows narrowed.

"Well, I hope you find that," she seemed to laugh at herself before tinkering with her bangles. "And I hope you'll find a family that values their heritage and tradition. It's important, you know, to be around people like you. Otherwise, the family is prone to all sorts of influences."

"Is that so?"

"Oh, yes," Mrs. Bharadwaj pontificated, quite eager to state her opinion. "It's all about a pure, clean environment."

"And I guess that's what attracted you to this flat? The pure and clean environment?"

"We noted its potential," Mrs. Bharadwaj said casually, eyes piercing Shonali.

All of a sudden, she felt as if she had entered the den of a predator. And perhaps it wasn't the men she should be anxious about meeting in this way. Mrs. Bharadwaj had a confidence about her that unsettled Shonali. The way she pushed out her chest, red lips smirking.

Shonali was certain Mrs. Bharadwaj was just as involved in the business as her husband, if not leading it directly. The woman knew Shonali was in a weakened state that she had no leverage.

"You were quite feminine earlier. Despite your... *dull* appearance, I was quite impressed with how dutiful you are toward your father. With the right direction, I thought you had potential as well."

"Are you suggesting I marry your son?"

"Not at all," Mrs. Bharadwaj shrugged. "Only, we're open to outsiders, compared to other families. The most important thing to us is *quality*. Good stock."

Shonali felt her stomach churn. She wanted to vomit her early lunch all over the table.

"It's really a good offer, considering," Mrs. Bharadwaj looked her up and down. "We're quite an ambitious family. We could even handle this flat for you."

"That's funny since you haven't been paying the rent. When you can easily afford it."

"As I've said, it was out of our control." The older woman smiled tightly. "But don't worry. Everything will be sorted out."

"I wonder who it will be sorted for. Does that mean I'll get the rent or something else?"

"What else would it mean?" Mrs. Bharadwaj's voice lowered, almost flat.

"I don't know. That's why I asked. It's a particular way to talk about paying due rent."

"Well, I'm a bit creative." Mrs. Bharadwaj relaxed, leaning back into her chair.

A silence descended over them. She wondered what 'sorted out' meant to a woman like Gita Bharadwaj. And she couldn't imagine anything good. It was clear that this was a business. Her brother had allowed in a force that did not care about the flat or the land or creating a better society or even housing their own family. Their sole focus was money.

Maybe they even got a kick out of exerting power over others.

Sitting in darkness, Shonali wanted to jump at every burst of thunder, every shudder of lightning. The tree whipped relentlessly against the window pane. And the roof continued to leak, more and more streams of water appearing in the paint.

The turn of a key alerted the two women to the front door. Mr. Bharadwaj and Arjun entered, their figures looming in the darkness. Closing the door behind them, the men did not remove their shoes. Arjun stayed close to the door.

"I'm afraid the bank is still held up. It's a government bank. What can you do?" Mr. Bharadwaj said, his dry tone betraying the seriousness of his gaze.

Shonali stood up hesitantly. The door was blocked.

"You said you had Rooh Afza, Mrs. Bharadwaj? Perhaps I should serve you all some. And we can discuss."

The offer took the three off-guard. While Mrs. Bharadwaj glared at her through narrowed eyes, her husband shrugged and finally removed his shoes. But Arjun did not. Instead, he leaned against the door, removing his phone, and feigned disinterest.

It would truly be a family affair, then.

Entering the kitchen, Shonali noticed a cockroach scurrying beneath the cupboards. A diya had burnt out, the peg of an incense stick dwindling in the wooden home temple at the entrance of the kitchen. Shonali found herself mumbling the Gayatri Mantra, the Hanuman Chalisa, anything to stay calm.

At the end of the day, her mildly malnourished frame was pitted against three healthy and heavy adults, two of them male and three times her size. She would need to be smart.

Clicking her tongue, she scrambled to find three glasses and poured Rooh Afza, and then water through the RO water filter.

But the scent of gas was strong, stronger than it had ever been. There had to be a leak.

She glanced back at the temple, noticing a matchbox at the edge of the platform. Frowning, Shonali tiptoed quietly to the template and pulled a match from the box. Returning to the stove, she lit one of the gas burners, careful to keep it on simmer. And then, with the three glasses, she returned to the room.

The positions had changed.

Mrs. Bharadwaj was near the door now, and Arjun was near the kitchen door. And the husband near the window, the most relaxed out of the two. Obviously, he planned to have the others take care of any physical confrontation.

Massaging his mustache, he watched as Shonali placed the tray of glasses before them. He took one in his hand but refused to drink it.

Shonali remained standing by the table.

"If you like, I can give you money to return home," Arjun said quietly. "I just got paid today, Shonali. You can just deduct it from what we owe."

Shonali turned toward him. While his voice was gentle, his eyes revealed a hidden hunger, an unspoken intention.

"That's very kind of you."

"I think it would be best."

"But it's been three months. Can you honestly say that the bank has held you all up for three months?"

"The account we use for rent, yes. I'm afraid we couldn't get the same money from the other accounts without jeopardizing business or our livelihood," Arjun said flatly.

"Even though your family company has bought other flats in the society?"

At this, he went rigid.

"That's Mr. Kapoor, the lawyer. Whoever said we bought flats got it mixed up," he said coldly.

Shonali paused. Wasn't the entity buying up flats at Padma Properties? Rudhrani seemed to suspect that Dilip Kapoor was involved, but not that it was definite.

"But he's your relative, isn't he? That's what you said when we met. Couldn't he lend you the money until the bank unfreezes the account?"

"He's lending us his time and expertise," Arjun bit back, taking a step forward. Shonali took a step back.

"If you own and rent flats, then you can understand my position," she responded, crossing her arms. She took a casual step away, further from the family and closer to the door.

"I don't work in that department of the business, sorry."

"Then you work in the hotel business?" The growing look of rage in his eyes revealed that he was more than tired of the conversation. He took another step forward. But Shonali held her ground.

"Look, I'll be frank, I don't care about this property at all."

At this, the air drained out of the room, and the rift of tension broke.

"You can keep it. But I want you all to leave my family alone, with the Pune flat. I know that a man visited my father and took his thumbprint as a signature. And I know they must be related to you."

Mr. Bharadwaj's face was indecipherable, emotionless. Shonali could feel all of their burning eyes.

"I'm afraid it doesn't matter what you care about or not," Mrs. Bharadwaj said firmly from her spot at the door. "The fact is, you couldn't take care of this flat. You could barely handle your own in Pune. As I said earlier, you need direction."

"And you're going to help with that?"

"We can take care of everything," the woman said confidently.

"Shut up, woman," her husband's voice boomed. Shonali heard him shift on the divan, heaving himself up.

"Miss Chatterjee. There's really nothing to be afraid of. Your father simply agreed to our help."

"He's incapacitated. He can't give consent," Shonali flew back, anger hot at her neck.

"He looked agreeable, from what I heard," Arjun shrugged.

"What happened to Mrs. Khan?"

At this, the family grew still. Mr. Bharadwaj's lips pursed into a thin, hard line, but his son appeared to relax, a dark glint in his eyes.

"Was she also agreeable?" Shonali spat out. "Or the watchman? Or my uncle?"

Mrs. Bharadwaj snorted in the corner, her white teeth glinting beneath her red lips. The pristine, thick kajal around her eyes could not contain the shadows of her glee, the forced presentation of politeness.

Then, Arjun suddenly loomed over her. "Shonali, I think maybe you should leave," he said almost calmly.

"Will you let me leave?"

"We aren't gangsters," Arjun retorted. "You can leave. But understand, you have to play by the rules."

"I'm pretty sure the rules say you can't just take my father's signature."

"Then you'll sign in his stead," Arjun flashed his teeth at her. In the flush of lightning, he looked like a demon standing before her, hulking and ready to pounce.

"Not for the Pune house."

"For both."

"Why do you need both? Isn't that greedy?" Shonali could see the restraint in Arjun weakening as his fists tightened at his sides.

"It's not just about the money."

"Isn't it?"

Shonali knew better. The Pune house, which her father had used his entire savings and a loan to purchase it for thirty lakhs, was now well worth more than a crore, more than 10,000,000 rupees. And it was in better condition than his little one-bedroom flat. For the Bharadwajs, it was a two-for-one deal.

"No. It's about the people, the environment," he said, his words mirroring his mother's.

Shonali clicked her tongue. She needed to make a decision. To placate them to be able to leave. But her agreeing with them would also be recorded if the phone in her pocket could even pick up their muffled conversations. And that would be shooting herself in the foot.

"Shonali, we're cleaning up, don't you understand?" Mrs. Bharadwaj interjected. "Besides, you don't even own this house properly."

"Be quiet," her husband shushed her again before approaching the door. All three were before her now.

"It was the seventies, eighties. Who had proper papers at that time?" Shonali bit back. It wasn't exactly wrong. But it wouldn't hold up in court.

"Shonali, you have to see our side. It's our business to make things better," Arjun said, puffing his chest out. "There are too many degenerates. Living next to them dirties your own home. Think of it as letting someone live next to you who doesn't shower, eats meat, or lets insects fester in their home. They tend to be like roaches themselves, like your uncle, your father. And then, before you know it, your own home is dirty. Then look how we've cleaned up everything. Isn't it so much better now? When you have high-quality people living next to you? People who hold the same values, the same level of cleanliness?"

"What would you know about my uncle? Or my father?" Perhaps she shouldn't have responded. These people were mad. Bloody mad. Far more than she had realized coming in. Rudhrani had been right—approaching them directly was dangerous.

Then it happened.

A light blasted into the dark room in an instant, heat erupting from the kitchen. Mrs. Bharadwaj screamed as a lick of fire swept into the hall and latched onto her sari.

Seeing her chance, Shonali flung herself past Arjun and his mother and swung the front door open. Screams followed behind her, and she joined the chorus, shouting fire as she raced down the stairs.

Behind her, Shonali could hear heavy footsteps nearly clamping down on her heels. A hand grabbed her hair harshly, pulling her backward on the stairs.

With all of her strength, Shonali slammed her foot against the assailant's toes and elbowed him in the stomach. With a grunt, his grip loosened, and she broke free, but not before his large hand reached out again. Pushing him weakly in the chest, Arjun slipped and fell behind, a crack echoing off the halls. She heard Mrs. Bharadwaj screech again at the top of the stairs.

On the second floor, Mrs. Kabraji was shaking at the door, eyes wide, an umbrella in her hand. Shonali grabbed the woman by the arm and rushed her down the stairs, voice hoarse and unable to answer the older woman's questions and complaints. She raced the woman across the car park into the second building.

Shonali watched the building burn, waiting for the Bharadwajs to stumble into the open air in anger as their investment crumbled in the flames. But they never emerged from the stairwell.

She could hear the roar of the fire as the glass window of her flat combusted, the red flames licking up the wet building walls, golden and emboldened.

The storm evaporated into a light drizzle as she stood there, simply staring. Sirens blared in the distance.

But for the first time, even as the blazing tower engulfed the sky, the billowing smoke merging with the curling blanket of clouds, Shonali felt free.

Chapter 23
The Beginning

Shonali poured a cup of chai, watching the waterfall of reddish-brown malai[1] cling to the edges of the strainer. She had splurged on adding cardamom and cinnamon powder, partly for her guest but mostly for herself.

"Do you need help?" Rudhrani asked from the living room.

"No, I've got it. Just one second," Shonali said. With one hand, she held a tray with two small cups. On the other was an array of dried fruits and biscuits. "I can't believe it's already Diwali in a few days. The last month has gone by fast."

"I can imagine. Thanks for this," Rudhrani said, coughing into her sleeve.

"Are you sick?" Shonali said, glancing at the investigator. "You never did explain that. You cough a lot."

"I have cystic fibrosis," Rudhrani said flatly. "It's a chronic illness. No need to worry about it."

"I'm so sorry."

"Don't be," Rudhrani waved her off. "I was supposed to die at ten or eleven, and I'm still here, aren't I? And you are, too, after all

---

1. Malai - The creamy layer of milk that forms when you boil it.

that." The woman leaned back and took a sip of tea. "I saw the rangoli outside. Very talented."

"Well, after finally landing a new job and caring for Dad, I needed something for myself. I'll now be a junior in marketing at a big multinational firm. I'd still like to get my master's, but with needing money, my father, and work, it won't be possible right now."

"But the job is good news," Rudhrani said cheerfully. "And the flat? Did you at least have insurance on the flat in Mumbai?"

"No, my father never paid for it," Shonali said, rolling her eyes. "But I don't care. In a desparation sale, I've gotten rid of the plot with Amar's help, our old broker. I wanted to be done with it, once and for all. That money got us through. Someone wanted to redevelop the land, so I got a few lakhs for it."

"I can imagine," Rudhrani said. "But I do have a lot to share with you. The conclusion of all this paperwork research." The detective wrinkled her nose and put her tea down on the table.

"Yes, well. My father and his brother, Sujoy, fought over the flat, I assumed. And obviously, Sujoy knew the Bharadwajs. I'm guessing he told them something while drunk. So, they made us a part of their squat-and-steal scam. Is that close to the truth?"

"Close but not quite," said Rudhrani. "Thanks to my uncle and his friends in the police force, we found a treasure trove of illegal documentation," she started. "Complaints, land taken under suspicious circumstances, mostly from elderly folks, but also farmers and so on. A whole racket across the state. And some in UP, too.

"Of course, under the guise of Padma Properties, they would redevelop the land, sell it to higher bidders, rent it—a few different money-making options. We're still digging, but I wouldn't be surprised if the properties were also used to launder black money. The case has been moved to the CBI[2]. It'll take time before the extent of the damage is revealed."

"And Mrs. Khan? Asha said you found her a few days ago—"

"Yes, she was alive. Honestly, I wasn't expecting she would be! Once the police got involved, it was possible to search the city far more effectively.

"She had been hit over the head and was found in a ditch near the Dhavari slums a few days after she disappeared. Nazia had been hit so hard that she didn't know where she was or even who she was. Would have died if it hadn't been for some kind soul taking her to the local clinic. We managed to find her panhandling. Her memory is still slowly coming back, but she'll need a lot of time to recover."

"Asha did say she was coming back to take care of her," said Shonali. "I'm still amazed she's alive. How did it happen, exactly?"

"About Mrs. Khan? I'm not entirely sure. I'm assuming they physically assaulted her and dumped her, expecting her to die of her wounds. I suppose we can be lucky your tenants were probably too arrogant to check. Oh, and that watchman was fine, too, after enough bed rest. Head wound. Probably the same kind of blunt attack from behind with a rock."

There was then, briefly, a pregnant pause before Rudhrani spoke again.

"I also contacted your aunt. I understand she wouldn't talk to you?"

Shonali nodded, somewhat ashamed. The woman blamed her for her uncle's death, and she couldn't exactly correct her.

---

2. CBI - Central Bureau of Investigation, a central government crime branch

"One thing I didn't tell you in the beginning was that I spoke to your uncle. He's the one who told Kapoor about your flat, about the tenuous paperwork and his intent to get it back. But he wouldn't explain *why* your father kicked him out in the first place.

"Luckily for us, he left a journal. And, after saying I was an investigator and showing off my uncle's track record, she let me see it. It's very detailed. And... and pretty dark. I came here to ask if you wanted to hear it. But keep in mind, you may think of your family differently."

"I'd rather know who they really are. Or were. I'm sick of being kept in the dark," said Shonali.

Not knowing had put her into this mess. It was better to be uncomfortable with the truth than try to hide from it.

"Okay. Good. So," Rudhrani mumbled as she opened her purse and fished out a bundle of diaries. "Here are the key entries. He started writing them after he discovered he had cancer. I guess the guilt kept gnawing at him. In these entries, he alleges that he and your father murdered your eldest uncle over ownership of the flat shortly after your grandfather passed away. Some restless gambler who apparently turned his life around and returned home."

Shonali stilled. She remembered her grandfather's funeral, the white sheets, and the marigold. It happened just before that summer with the fly infestation. Yet, she couldn't remember her eldest uncle at all.

"They killed him together, but apparently your uncle was supposed to get rid of the body, which took some time. They kept him in your flat for the first two days, but he managed to drop it in a landfill.

"Over time, they squabbled about the upkeep and inheritance, and of course, your father, having the advantage of being sober, won out."

Shonali was silent. She wasn't sure how to feel or how to process the information. Her father, a murderer?

And yet, a part of her knew it must be the truth. That damned summer, with its damned insect infestation. The same year, her grandfather passed, and her father's brother disappeared. She could remember the rotting smell, which she had always attributed to the heat and the bugs. Then she remembered her father's anger, often explosive towards his brother, sometimes her mother. His envious eyes were on the neighbors' cars and parties. How he bragged about his children as if their accomplishments were his own.

Her stomach churned. How much of a prize it must have been to be able to brag about having a second flat. About a second flat in Mumbai. About the illusion of wealth.

And still, Shonali realized she would never know the full truth. With his paralysis, her father would die, unable to confess to or deny the crime.

Her uncle, at least, had kept a record. It would explain the estrangement, the hatefulness that swelled between the two. And how easy a target their greed had made her.

"So, then, Sujoy Uncle told them about us, about the flat. And my brother probably peppered in the rest. And they realized we were good candidates for their scam. That they could take the Pune house, too, with enough forethought," said Shonali, placing her demitasse on the coffee table.

Horrible people. Her exhaustion had led her to see them as demons, treating her as a cat paw at a mouse—enjoying a kill. And yet they were not mythological beings, only convincing ones, preying on the weakness of others.

Despite their crimes, their passing was barely noted. A blip in the news cycle. The reports listed a gas leak as the cause of the fire, and the official investigators were only too eager to close the case of their deaths. Whether that was due to Rudhrani's connections or because of the desire to focus on the living remaining conman, Dilip Kapoor, she couldn't be sure.

"I guess so," Rudhrani shrugged. "Knowledge is power. And most people don't have the expertise or finances to keep up with real estate. So, it's easy to take land with minimum risk if you know what you're doing. They knew it, and they knew it would be difficult for you to manage. Difficult for your elderly neighbors to deal with, too."

Shonali frowned and stared at the plate full of biscuits, her stomach too uneasy to partake.

"I'm planning to start fresh. Completely," she finally said softly.

"I don't blame you," Rudhrani chuckled, crossing her legs. "You basically went through a trial by fire over here. And your brother, he'll help?"

"He's useless," Shonali said. "I don't need him. I don't want his money. And I don't want his advice. I want to do things on my own terms."

Rudhrani nodded. "There probably wasn't much he could do from abroad. I hope you're not too hard on him."

"I wasn't asking him to come back," Shonali said, eyes wet. Gingerly, she placed the tea saucer on the table. "I just wanted him to care."

They spoke throughout the afternoon till dusk, and then Shonali found herself alone again, looking out from the balcony at a sea of city lights. From Primpi-Chinchwad and Koregaon Park, all the way across the sprawling city to her little housing society, the sky glowed brightly.

Eventually, Rudhrani left. Shonali tended to her father and began to clean up, wondering where the time had gone.

Washing the cups and tucking away the sweets, Shonali worked in pleasant solitude. The past two months—the police investigation, the death of the Bharadwajs in the flat—all of it had given her anxiety. But not nearly as much as she had been in those few days at the Golden Deer Housing Society, handling her untenable inheritance.

For now, the past was finally finished. The flat was gone, but she had never wanted it. She had cursed it, and its bloody history had, in turn, cursed her.

Shonali heard, from the balcony, a crow cawing, its beady eyes staring at her from its perch on the railing. Removing a round piece of dough from the fridge, she tossed it out into the night. Her little visitor picked it up with its beak, stared at her blankly, and waited until she turned to fly away.

More Rudhrani Sen

RUDHRANI SEN MYSTERIES

A Murder in the Garden of Dreams (Get it for free in the newsletter)
Missing in Mumbai

GET MORE FREEBIES AND DISCOUNTS:

kirkiakrivou.com/newsletter

Acknowledgments

This book wouldn't be possible without the amazing support of my family and friends, as well as the input, critiques, and editing from Jaenelle Shiroshita, Mis Hashmi, Guntaas Chugh, Vidhipssa Mohan, Danai Christopoulou, Ankita B, and many other contributors and readers. And of course, thank you to Sejuti Bala, who designed a fabulous illustration for this story. Thank you all so much!

About Author

Kirki Akrivou is a Greek-American author. When not writing mystery novels, you can find her traveling, reading, or just nerding out about history.

Website: www.kirkiakrivou.com

Twitter:
https://twitter.com/KirkiAkrivou

TikTok: https://www.tiktok.com/@kirkiakrivou